W.H.G Kingston

Adventures in Africa

W.H.G Kingston

Adventures in Africa

1st Edition | ISBN: 978-3-75237-168-0

Place of Publication: Frankfurt am Main, Germany

Year of Publication: 2020

Outlook Verlag GmbH, Germany.

W.H.G. Kingston

"Adventures in Africa"

Chapter One.

"How many more days, Jan, will it be before we get across this abominable desert?" I asked of our black guide, as we trudged along, he leading our sole remaining ox, while my uncle, Mr Roger Farley, and I led our two horses laden with the remnants of our property.

"May be ten days, may be two ten," answered Jan Jigger, whose knowledge of numerals was somewhat limited.

I gave a groan, for I was footsore and weary, and expected to have had a more satisfactory answer. We were making our way over a light-coloured soft sand, sprinkled in some places with tall grass, rising in tufts, with bare spots between them. In other parts were various creeping plants, and also—though I called the region a desert—there were extensive patches of bushes, above which here and there rose clumps of trees of considerable height. This large amount of vegetation, however, managed to exist without streams or pools, and for miles and miles together we had met with no water to quench our own thirst or that of our weary beasts. My uncle was engaged in the adventurous and not unprofitable occupation of trading with the natives in the interior of Africa. He had come down south some months before to dispose of the produce of his industry at Graham's Town, where I had joined him, having been sent for from England. After purchasing a fresh supply of goods, arms, powder, and shot, and giving a thorough repair to his waggons, he had again set off northward for the neighbourhood of lake Ngami, where he was to meet his partner, Mr Welbourn, who had with him his son Harry, with whom I had been at school, and who was about my own age. We had, beyond the borders of the colony, been attacked by a party of savages, instigated by the Boers, two or three of whom indeed led them. They had deprived us of our cattle and men, we having escaped with a small portion only of our goods, two of our horses, a single ox and our one faithful Bechuana. To get away from our enemies we had taken a route unusually followed across the Kalahari desert. We were aware of the dangers and difficulties to be encountered, but the road was much shorter than round either to the east or west; and though we knew that wild animals abounded, including elephants, rhinoceroses, lions, leopards, and hyaenas, yet we believed that we should be able to contend with them, and that we should not be impeded by human savages. Day after day we trudged forward. The only water we could obtain was by digging into certain depressions in the ground which our guide pointed out, when, having scraped

"WATER COME SOON. WATER COME SOON!"

out the sand with the single spade we possessed and our hands, we arrived at a hard stratum, beyond which he advised us not to go. In a short time the water began to flow in slowly, increasing by degrees until we had enough for ourselves and our cattle.

We had now, however, been travelling sixty miles or more, without finding one of these water-holes; and though we had still a small quantity of the precious liquid for ourselves, our poor horses and ox had begun to suffer greatly. Still Jan urged us to go forward.

"Water come soon, water come soon!" he continued saying, keeping his eye ranging about in every direction in search of the expected hole.

Trusting to Jan's assurances, thirst compelled us to consume the last drop of our water. Still, hour after hour went by, and we reached no place at which we could replenish it. Our sufferings became terrible. My throat felt as if seared by a hot iron. Often I had talked of being thirsty, but I had never before known what thirst really was. My uncle, I had no doubt, was suffering as much as I was, but his endurance was wonderful.

We had seen numbers of elands sporting round us in every direction, but as soon as we approached them, off they bounded.

"Surely those deer do not live without water; it cannot be far away," I observed.

"They are able to pass days and weeks without tasting any," said my uncle. "They can besides quickly cover thirty or forty miles of ground if they wish to reach it. We must try to shoot one of them for supper, which may give us both meat and drink. See, in the wood yonder we can leave our horses and the ox under Jan's care, and you and I will try to stalk one of the animals."

On reaching the wood, my uncle and I, with our guns in our hands, took a direction which would lead us to leeward of the herd, so that we might not be scented as we approached.

By creeping along under the shelter of some low bushes as we neared them, the elands did not see us. Hunger and thirst made us unusually cautious and anxious to kill one. My uncle told me to reserve my fire, in case he should fail to bring the eland down; but as he was a much better shot than I was, I feared that should he miss, I also should fail. Presently I saw him rise from among the grass. Lifting his rifle to his shoulder he fired; the eland gave a bound, but alighting on its feet was scampering off, when I eagerly raised my rifle and pulled the trigger. As the smoke cleared off, to my infinite delight I saw the eland struggling on the grass. We both rushed forward, and my uncle's knife quickly deprived it of life. It was a magnificent animal, as big as an ox, being the largest of the South African antelopes.

On opening its stomach we discovered water, which, on being allowed to cool, was sufficiently pure to quench our burning thirst. We secured a portion of it for Jan, and loading ourselves with as much meat as we could carry, we returned to where we had left him. A fire was soon lighted, and we lost no time in cooking a portion of the flesh. With our thirst partially relieved we were able to eat. We had made our fire at some distance from the shrubs for fear of igniting them, while we tethered our horses and ox among the longest grass we could find. In that dry region no shelter was required at night, so we lay down to sleep among our bales, with our saddles for pillows, and our rifles by our sides. I had been sleeping soundly, dreaming of purling streams and babbling fountains, when I awoke to find my throat as dry and parched as ever. Hoping to find a few drops of water in my bottle, I sat up to reach for it; when, as I looked across the fire, what was my dismay to see a large tiger-like animal stealthily approaching, and tiger I fully believed it to be. On it came, exhibiting a pair of round bright shining eyes. I expected every moment to see it spring upon us. I was afraid that by crying out I might only hasten its movements, so I felt for my rifle and, presenting at the creature's head shouted—

"A tiger, uncle; a tiger, Jan!"

"A tiger!" exclaimed my uncle, springing up in a moment. "That's not a tiger, it's a leopard, but if pressed by hunger may prove as ugly a customer. Don't fire until I tell you, for if wounded it will become dangerous."

All this time the leopard was crawling on, though it must have heard the sound of our voices; perhaps the glare of the fire in its eyes prevented it from seeing us, for it still cautiously approached. I saw my uncle lift his rifle; he fired, but though his bullet struck the creature, instead of falling as I expected, it gave a bound and the next instant

"A TIGER, UNCLE; A TIGER, JAN!"

would have been upon us. Now was my time. As it rose, I fired, and my bullet must have gone through its heart, for over it rolled without a struggle, perfectly dead.

"Bravo! Fred," exclaimed my uncle. "This is the second time within a few hours your rifle has done good service. You'll become a first-rate hunter if you go on as you've begun. How that leopard came here it's difficult to say, unless it was driven from the hills, and has been wandering over the desert in search of prey; those creatures generally inhabit a high woody country."

Jan exhibited great delight at our victory, and having made up the fire, we spent some time in skinning the beast. Its fur was of great beauty, and although it would add to the load of our ox, we agreed to carry it with us, as it would be a welcome present to any chief who might render us assistance.

Having flayed the animal and pegged down the skin, we returned to our beds, hoping to finish the night without interruption. As soon as there was light sufficient to enable us to see our way, we pushed

5

forward, earnestly praying that before the sun was high in the heavens, we might fall in with water. Notwithstanding that Jan repeatedly exclaimed, "Find water soon! Find water soon!" not a sign of it could we see. A glare from a cloudy sky was shed over the whole scene; clumps of trees and bushes looking so exactly alike, that after travelling several miles, we might have fancied that we had made no progress. At length even the trees and bushes became scarcer, and what looked like a veritable desert appeared before us.

I had gone on a short distance ahead, when to my delight I saw in front a large lake, in the centre of which the waves were dancing and sparkling in the sunlight, the shadows of the trees being vividly reflected on the mirror-like surface near the shores, while beyond I saw what I took to be a herd of elephants flapping their ears and intertwining their trunks.

"Water, water!" I shouted; "we shall soon quench our thirst. We must take care to avoid those elephants, however," I added, pointing them out to my uncle. "It would be a fearful thing to be charged by them."

The horses and ox lifted up their heads and pressed forward. Jan to my surprise said nothing, though I knew he was suffering as well as my uncle and I were. I was rushing eagerly forward, when suddenly a haze which hung over the spot, broke and dispelled the illusion. A vast salt-pan lay before us. It was covered with an effervescence of lime, which had produced the deceptive appearance. Our spirits sank lower than ever. To avoid the salt-pan, we turned to the right, so as to skirt its eastern side. The seeming elephants proved to be zebras, which scampered off out of reach. We now began to fear that our horses would give in, and that we should have to push forward with our ox alone, abandoning everything it could not carry. Still my uncle cried "Forward!" Jan had evidently mistaken the road, and passed the spot where he had expected to find water. Still he observed that we need have no fear of pursuing our course. Evening was approaching and we must again camp: without water we could scarcely expect to get through the night.

Presently Jan looking out ahead, darted forward and stopped at where a small plant grew with linear leaves and a stalk not thicker than a crow's quill. Instantly taking a spade fastened to the back of the ox, he began eagerly digging away; and after he had got down to the depth of a foot, he displayed to us a tuber, the size of an enormous turnip. On removing the rind, he cut it open with his axe, and showed us a mass of cellular tissue filled up with a juicy substance which he handed to us, and applying a piece to his own mouth ate eagerly away at it. We imitated his example, and were almost immediately much refreshed. We found several other plants of the same sort, and digging up the roots gave them to the horses and ox, who crunched them up with infinite satisfaction.

Our thirst was relieved in a way I could scarcely have supposed possible. The animals too, trudged forward with far lighter steps than before. Relieved of our thirst and in the hopes of finding either water or more tubers next morning, we lay down thankful that we had escaped the fearful danger we had apprehended. As we advanced we looked out anxiously for the tuber-bearing plants, but not one could we see. I had gone on some little distance ahead, when I caught sight of a round object some way off, which, as the rays of sun fell on it, appeared of scarlet hue. I ran towards it, when I saw what looked like a small oblong red melon.

"Here's something worth having!" I exclaimed, cutting into it with my knife. When I applied it to my mouth, to my disappointment I found that, although juicy in the extreme, it was perfectly bitter. I threw it down in disgust. Jan soon afterwards, on coming near, said:

"Dis no good, but find oders presently!"

Hurrying along, he struck one after another, and quickly handed me one perfectly sweet; when he collected many more, with which we returned to where my uncle had halted with the animals.

The fruit was far more gratifying to the taste than the tubers. We allowed the animals to eat as many as they wished, and, loading them with a supply in case we should fail to find others further on, we continued our journey.

Those melons lasted us another whole day and a night, and afforded the only liquid which passed our mouths. As we were on foot our view over the level desert was limited.

I was walking alongside my uncle, discussing our future plans, having begun to hope that, in spite of the difficulties we had to contend against, we should get through, when I saw some objects moving rapidly in the distance. They were coming towards us.

"They are ostriches!" cried my uncle; "we must try and kill a few to obtain their plumes."

We halted, and remained perfectly still, hoping that the birds might approach us. Now they ran as fleet as a race-horse, now they stopped and went circling round. Two or three odd-looking birds, as they seemed, were moving at a much slower rate.

"Those Bosjeemen!" cried Jan.

We at length saw that the latter were human beings, their legs covered with white pigment and carrying the head and feathers of an ostrich on their backs, while each had in his hand a bow and a number of arrows. Presently they cautiously approached the ostriches to leeward, stopping every now and then and pretending to be feeding. The ostriches would look at the strange birds, but, not suspecting danger, allowed them to approach. One of the Bosjeemen then shot an arrow, when the wounded bird and his companions ran off; the former, however, quickly dropped, when the other birds stopped to see what was the matter, and thus allowed their enemy to draw near enough to shoot another arrow.

In this way three little yellow-skinned fellows each shot, in a short time, four magnificent ostriches. They had seen us in the distance, but instead of running away, as we feared they would do, one of them, guessing we were traders, came forward to bargain for the sale of the feathers, and Jan acting as interpreter, my uncle expressed a willingness to trade. The Bosjeemen then produced a number of reeds, scarcely the thickness of my little finger. Having plucked off the feathers, they pushed them into the reeds; and, thus preserved, the feathers were fit to travel any distance without being spoilt.

It was late by the time the whole operation was performed, and we had given the articles they had agreed to take in exchange. As the reeds weighed but little, the loads were considerably lightened.

Jan now explained to our new friends that they would be further rewarded if they would conduct us to water. They at once agreed to do so, and one of them, hurrying away to a spot at a distance where they had left their travelling equipage, returned with a dozen ostriches' eggs in a net at his back; he then made a sign to us to follow him, while his companions remained with the ostriches they had shot. Sooner than we expected he reached a hole, into which he rapidly dug with his hand; then, inserting a long reed, he began to suck away with might and main. In a short time the water flowed, and was led down by another reed into a hole at the end of an ostrich egg, which was soon filled with water. As we had a leathern bucket we were enabled to give our animals a drink, though we could not allow them as much as they would have liked.

The Bosjeeman then, refilling the egg-shells, returned with us to where we had left his companions. We found that they had built themselves a hut, if so it could be called, in a thick mimosa bush, by bending the boughs so as to form a roof, covered by reeds lightly fastened together. The inside was lined with dried leaves, grass, and the coarser feathers of the ostrich. When they saw that we were encamped, the three hunters lighted a fire and sat themselves down before it to enjoy a sumptuous repast of ostrich flesh. Though unattractive in appearance, they were honest little fellows, and we slept in perfect security, knowing that they would give us timely notice of the approach of an enemy.

Jan assured us that we might trust them, as it was a high mark of confidence on their part to show us

" THOSE BOSJEEMEN !" CRIED JAN.   [p. 13.

where we could procure water, for they are always careful to hide such spots from those they think unfriendly.

They accompanied us the following day, and led us to a pool, the only one we had met with while crossing the desert. Probably in many seasons that also would have been empty. Here our animals got as much water as they could drink, and we filled our water-bottles. We then parted from our yellow friends, who said that, as they were ignorant of the country to the northward, they could not venture farther. Trusting to Jan's sagacity to find water, we proceeded in good spirits.

We had hoped to trade largely with the natives, but as we had lost the greater part of our goods, we should have to depend upon our own exertions to obtain the ivory and skins which would repay us for the difficulties and dangers of our journey. We had fortunately saved the greater part of our ammunition, which would enable us to hunt for some months to come.

Of course we knew Mr Welbourn would be much disappointed at seeing us arrive with so slender an equivalent for the skins and ivory my uncle had taken south, instead of the waggon full of goods which he had expected.

"He is a sensible, good-natured fellow, and will know that it was from no fault of ours we were plundered," observed my uncle. "We shall still do well, and shall probably encounter more adventures than we should have met with had we confined ourselves to simple trading with the natives. I should, however, have preferred that to undergoing the fatigues of hunting; besides which we might the sooner have returned with our cargo of ivory to the coast."

Several more days passed by during which we came to three spots where we were able to obtain a sufficient amount of water to satisfy ourselves and our thirsty animals. Sometimes for miles together not a drop could be procured, and had it not been for the tubers, and the little red melons I have described, the horses and our patient ox must have perished. At length the sheen of water in the bright sunlight was seen in the distance. This time we were convinced that it was not a mirage. We pushed forward, hoping that our sufferings from thirst were at an end. Trees of greater height than any we had yet met with since leaving the colony fringed the banks of a fine river. On examining the current we found that it was flowing to the north-east, and we therefore hoped that by following it up we should reach the lake for which we were bound. Our black guide, however, advised that we should cross the river, which was here fordable, and by steering north, considerably shorten the journey. On wading through the water we looked out sharply for crocodiles and hippopotami, lest one of those fresh-water monsters should venture to attack us; we got over, however, without accident. Having allowed our animals to drink their full of water, and replenished our bottles, we encamped for the night under a magnificent *baobab* tree with a trunk seventy feet in girth as high as we could reach, while our animals found an abundance of rich grass on which to satisfy their hunger.

"THE THREE HUNTERS LIGHTED A FIRE AND SAT THEMSELVES DOWN BEFORE IT." [A. 14

What pigmies we felt as we stood beneath that giant tree. An army might have found shelter from the sun under its wide-spreading boughs. We thought the spot a perfect paradise after our long journey across the plain.

We had not long been seated round our camp-fire, when Jan made a dart at his foot and caught a fly which had settled on it; and, exhibiting it to my uncle, exclaimed—

"No good, no good!"

It was of a brownish colour with three yellow bars across the body, and scarcely larger than a common house-fly. We soon saw others buzzing about in considerable numbers.

I asked Jan what he meant.

"Das de *tsetse*: when bite horse or ox den dey die," he answered.

As, however, neither my uncle nor I felt any ill effects from the bites of the flies, we thought that Jan must be mistaken, and at all events it was now too late to shift our encampment. We therefore, having made up a blazing fire to scare off any wild beasts, lay down to sleep, without thinking more of the flies, which did not cause us any annoyance.

The next morning we saw some of the creatures on the legs of our horses and the ox; but we soon brushed them away, and, loading up, we continued our journey. They went on as usual. Jan, however, looked much disconcerted, and I saw him continually brushing off the flies.

"No good, no good!" he said, "hope soon get through, for de horses not

11

go far."

I asked my uncle what Jan meant. He replied that he had often heard of the tsetse fly, but never having passed through a country infested by it, he was disinclined to believe the stories told of the deadly effects of its bite on cattle and horses.

Chapter Two.

We soon passed through the tsetse district, which was not more than a couple of miles wide, and, as our animals showed no appearance of suffering, we hoped that they had escaped injury.

We had determined to encamp early in the day near a pool fed by a rivulet which fell into the main stream, in order that we might shoot some game for our supper. Leaving Jan in charge of the camp, my uncle and I set off, believing that we could easily find our way back to the fire. We had gone some distance when we caught sight of a herd of antelopes. In order that we might have a better chance of killing one of them, my uncle told me to make a wide circuit, keeping to leeward of the deer towards a clump of trees, whence I might be able to get a favourable shot, while he lay down concealed by the brushwood near where we then were.

Taking advantage of all the bushes and trunks of trees on the way, I approached the antelopes without disturbing them. Looking out from the cover I had gained, I watched the beautiful creatures, hoping that one of them would come within range of my rifle. It

"WHAT WAS MY SURPRISE TO SEE A HUGE LION!" [*p.* 15.

was tantalising to see them feeding so quietly just out of my reach. Still, though I might not get a shot, I hoped that they might go off towards where my uncle was lying hid. Presently, however, they bounded towards me; and, thinking it possible that they might again turn, I fired at one of the leading animals, which, notwithstanding its wound, still went on, though at slackened speed. Instead of reloading, as I ought to have done, I dashed forward to secure it. Scarcely, however, had I left my cover than what was my surprise, and I must confess my dismay, to see a huge lion! Should I attempt to escape by flight, the savage brute would, I knew, follow me. I fixed my eyes as steadily as I could upon him, while I attempted to reload. At the same time I knew that, even should I fire, I might only wound him, when he would become more fierce. There were trees near, up which it was possible I might climb should he give me time, but it was not likely that he would do that. I wondered that he did not pursue the antelope; but probably he had lately had his dinner, or he certainly would have done so. I continued loading, he lashing his tail and roaring furiously. I expected every moment that he would spring upon me. To escape by any other way than by shooting him dead seemed impossible.

I finished loading, and brought my gun up ready to fire. Should I miss or only wound him, he would be upon me in a moment. I had hitherto remained quite silent, but it occurred to me that if I should shout loudly enough my uncle would hear my cry for help. I thought, too, that I might scare the lion. When once I had made up my mind to shout, I did so with might and main.

I was answered by a distant "hollo!" by which I knew that my uncle was still a long way off. He would, however, understand that I was in danger, and come to my assistance; or, if too late to help me, would provide for his own safety.

The lion seemed as undecided how to act as I was. As I shouted he roared, and again lashed his tail, but did not advance a step. This gave me courage; but, although the monarch of the forest did not appear in a combative mood, I felt very sure that, should I wound him, his rage would be excited. I dared not for a moment withdraw my eye from him, and thus we stood regarding each other. To me it seemed a prodigiously long time. At last he seemed to lose patience, for his roars became more frequent and louder and louder, and he lashed his tail more furiously. I raised my rifle to my shoulder. He came on at a cat-like pace, evidently ignorant of the power of the weapon I held in my hands. In another instant he would spring at me. I pulled the trigger. To my horror, the cap failed to ignite the powder. I saw the monstrous brute in the act of springing, but at the same moment I heard the crack of a rifle close to me; the next, a tremendous roar rent the air. I was felled to the earth, and felt myself weighed down by a vast body, unable to breathe or move. It was some time before I came to myself, when, looking up, I saw my uncle kneeling by my side.

"The lion very nearly did for you, Fred," he said; "but cheer up, lad. I don't think you're mortally hurt, though you've had a narrow squeak for it. Had your gun not missed fire, you might have shot the lion yourself. Here he lies, and there's the springbok."

While my uncle was talking, he was examining my hurts. The lion had given me a fearful blow with his paw, and had injured one of my shoulders. It was a wonder indeed that he did not kill me.

"We must get you to the camp somehow," said my uncle; "I cannot leave you here while I bring the ox, so the sooner we set off the better."

Taking me up in his arms, he began to stagger on with me; but, though he was a strong man, I was no slight weight, and he had great difficulty in getting along. I asked him to let me walk, as I thought that I could do so with his support. When I tried, however, I found that I could not move one foot before the other. As we got within hail of the camp he shouted to Jan to come and help him; and together they carried me along the remainder of the distance.

"Now that we have you safe here, though I am unwilling to leave you, I must go back and fetch the antelope, for we cannot do without food," he said.

Telling Jan to collect materials for building a hut, as it was evident that I should be unable to move for some time, and also charging him to keep an eye on me, he started off.

I felt a great deal of pain, but I retained my senses, and tried to divert my thoughts by watching Jan, who was busily employed in cutting long sticks and branches for the hut.

It seemed to me that my uncle had been gone for more than an hour, and I began to fear that some accident might have happened to him. Where there was one lion it was probable that there were others, and they might revenge themselves on the slayer of their relative.

Jan, however, kept working away as if satisfied that all was right, now and then taking a look at me, and throwing a few sticks on the fire to get it to burn brightly. He then began to prepare for roasting the expected venison by placing some uprights, with cross pieces to serve as spits, close to the fire.

"Hurrah! here am de Cap'n!" he at length shouted, such being the title he usually bestowed on my uncle. "He bring springbok, an' someting else too."

I felt greatly relieved when I saw my uncle throw down his heavy load, consisting not only of the antelope which I had shot, but of the lion's skin.

"I brought this," he said, "to make a bed for you. You want it, though it is not fit at present to serve the purpose."

I thanked him for his offer, but declared that I would rather just then be left where I was, as any movement pained me.

Jan lost no time in cutting off some pieces of venison, and placing them to roast. My uncle also put on a pot with a small portion to make some soup, which he said would suit me better than the roast. Hungry as I was, though I tried to eat some of the latter as soon as Jan declared it sufficiently done, I could not manage to get it down. My

thirst became excessive, and it was fortunate that we were near water, or I believe I should otherwise have died.

The hut was soon finished, and some leaves and grass placed in it for me to lie upon. The soup did me some good, but I suffered so much pain that I could scarcely sleep all the night, and in the morning was in so fevered a condition, that I was utterly unfit to travel. I was very sorry to delay my uncle, but it could not be helped, and he bore the detention with his usual good temper. Nothing could exceed his kindness. He sat by my side for hours together; he dressed my wounds whenever he thought it necessary, and indeed tended me with the greatest care.

Day after day, however, went by, and I still remained in the same helpless state. He would not have left me for a moment, I believe, but it was necessary to go out and procure more game.

Jan had undertaken to scrape and prepare the lion's skin. He was thus employed near the stream at a little distance from the camp when I was startled by hearing a loud snort; and, looking up, what was my horror to see him rushing along, with a huge hippopotamus following him! In another minute I expected to see him seized by its formidable jaws and trampled to death, and then I thought that the savage brute would make at me. In vain I attempted to rise and get my gun, but my uncle, when he went out, had forgotten to place it near me. I tried to cry out and frighten the brute, but I could not raise my voice sufficiently high. Poor Jan shrieked loud enough, but his cries had no effect on the monster. He was making for a tree, up which he might possibly have climbed, when his feet slipped, and over he rolled on the ground. He was now perfectly helpless, and in a few minutes the hippopotamus would trample him to death. It seemed as if all hope was gone; but, at the very instant that I thought poor Jan's death was certain, my uncle suddenly appeared, when, aiming behind the ear of the hippopotamus, he fired, and the monster fell. Jan narrowly escaped being crushed, which he would have been had he not by a violent effort rolled out of the way.

Suffering as I was, I could scarcely help laughing at Jan's face, as, getting up on his knees, he looked with a broad grin at the hippopotamus, still uncertain whether it was dead or not. At length, convinced that his enemy could do him no further harm, he rose to his feet, exclaiming—

"Tankee, tankee, cap'n! If de gun not go off, Jan no speak 'gain."

Then, hurrying on, he examined the creature, to be certain that no life remained in it.

"What we do wid dis?" he asked, giving the huge body a kick with his foot.

"As it will shortly become an unpleasant neighbour, we must manage to drag him away from the camp," observed my uncle. "If the stream were deep enough, I would drag it in, and let it float down with the current; but, as it would very likely get stranded close to us, we must haul it away with the ox and the horses, though I doubt if the animals will like being thus employed."

I thought the plan a good one; and my uncle told Jan to catch the horses and ox, while he contrived some harness with the ropes and straps used for securing their cargoes. The ox showed perfect indifference to the dead hippopotamus, but the horses were very unwilling to be harnessed. They submitted, however, to act as leaders, while the ox had the creature's head, round which a rope was passed, close to its heels. Even then the animals found it no easy task to drag the huge body along over the rough ground.

"We shall not be long gone, Fred," said my uncle, placing a rifle and a brace of pistols close to me. "I hope that no other hippopotamus or lion or leopard will pay you a visit while we are away. If they do, you must use these, and I trust that you'll be able to drive off the creatures, whatever they may be."

I felt rather uncomfortable at being left alone in the camp, but it could not be helped; and I could only pray that another hippopotamus might not make its appearance. This one, in all probability, came up the stream far from its usual haunts.

I kept my rifle and pistols ready for instant use. The time seemed very long. As I listened to the noises in the forest, I fancied that I could hear the roaring and mutterings of lions, and the cries of hyaenas. Several times I took my rifle in my hand, expecting to see a lion stealing up to the camp. I caught sight in the distance of the tall necks of a troop of giraffes stalking across the country, followed soon afterwards by a herd of bounding blesboks, but no creatures came near me. At last my uncle and Jan returned with our four-footed attendants.

"We have carried the monster's carcase far enough off to prevent it from poisoning us by its horrible odour when it putrifies, which it will in a few hours," he observed. "But I am afraid that it will attract the hyaenas and jackals in no small numbers, so that we shall be annoyed by their howls and screechings. I am sorry to say also that the horses seem ill able to perform their work, and I greatly fear that they have been injured by the tsetse fly. If we lose them we shall have a difficulty in getting along. However, we won't despair until the evil day comes."

I should have said that my uncle, just before he rescued Jan from the hippopotamus, had shot another antelope, which he had brought to the camp, so that we were in no want of food.

Several days went by. Though I certainly was not worse, my recovery was very slow, and I was scarcely better able to travel than I was at first; though I told my uncle that I would try and ride if he wished to move on.

"I doubt if either of the horses can carry you," he answered. "Both are getting thin and weak, and have a running from their nostrils, which Jan says is the result of the tsetse poison. If you are better in a day or two we will try and advance to the next stream or water-hole; and perhaps we may fall in with natives, from whom we may purchase some oxen to replace our horses. It will be a great disappointment to lose the animals, for I had counted on them for hunting."

That night we were entertained by a concert of hideous howlings and cries, produced we had no doubt by the hyaenas and jackals; but by keeping up a good fire, and occasionally discharging our rifles, we prevented them from approaching the camp.

At the end of two days I fancied myself better. We accordingly determined the next morning to recommence our journey. At daybreak we breakfasted on the remains of the last deer shot, and my uncle having placed me on his horse, which was the stronger of the two, put part of its cargo on the other. Pushing on, we soon left behind the camp we had so long occupied.

On starting I bore the movement pretty well, and fancied that I should be able to perform the journey without difficulty. For the first two days, indeed, we got on better than I had expected, though I was thankful when the time for camping arrived. On the third morning I suffered much, but did not tell my uncle how ill I felt, hoping that I should recover during the journey. We had a wild barren tract to cross, almost as wild as the desert. The ox trudged on as patiently as ever, but the horses were very weak, and I had great difficulty in keeping mine on its legs. Several times it had stumbled, but I was fortunately not thrown off. Our pace, however, was necessarily very slow, and we could discover no signs of water, yet water we must reach before we could venture to camp.

Jan generally led the ox, while my uncle walked by my side, holding the rein of the other horse. Again and again my poor animal had stumbled; when, as my uncle was looking another way, down it came, and I was thrown with considerable violence to the ground.

My uncle, having lifted me up, I declared that I was not much hurt, and begged him to replace me on the horse. The poor animal was unable

"DAME WATER, DARE WATER!" [A. 38.

to rise. In vain Jan and he tried to get it on its legs. He and Jan took off the saddle and the remaining part of the load, but all was of no use. At last we came to the melancholy conclusion that its death was inevitable. Our fears were soon realised: after it had given a few struggles, its head sinking on the sand, it ceased to move. We had consequently to abandon some more of our heavier things, and having transferred the remaining cargo to the ox, my uncle put me on the back of the other

19

horse. Scarcely, however, had we proceeded a mile than down it came, and I was again thrown to the ground, this time to be more hurt than at first.

I bore the suffering as well as I could, and made no complaint, while my uncle and Jan tried to get the horse up. It was soon apparent, however, that its travelling days were done, and that we had now the ox alone to depend upon.

"I wish that I could walk," I said, but when I made the attempt I could not proceed a dozen paces. Had not my uncle supported me I should have sunk to the ground. We could not stay where we were, for both we and our poor ox required water and food.

"We must abandon our goods," said my uncle; "better to lose them than our lives. We will, however, if we can find a spot near here, leave them *en cache*, as the Canadian hunters say; and if we soon fall in with any friendly natives, we can send and recover them."

He had just observed, he said, a small cave, and he thought that by piling up some stones in front of it the things would remain uninjured from the weather or wild beasts for a considerable time.

As it was only a short distance off, while Jan remained with me, he led the ox to the spot. The cave, fortunately, had no inhabitant; and, having placed the goods within, and piled some stones so as completely to block up the entrance, he returned, retaining only the powder and shot, the ostrich feathers, three or four skins, our cooking utensils, a few packages of tea, coffee, sugar, pepper, and similar articles weighing but little. Unfortunately, in building up the wall, one of the larger stones had dropped, and severely injured his foot. He found it so painful that he was unable to walk. He, therefore, mounting the ox, took me up before him. I, indeed, by this time could not even hold on to the saddle, so had not he carried me I should have been unable to travel. We now once more went on. It was already late in the day, and before long darkness overtook us; still we could not stop without water, which we hoped, however, to find before long. In a short time the moon rose and enabled us to see our way.

The prospect was dreary in the extreme. Here and there a few trees sprang out of the arid soil, while on every side were rocks with little or no vegetation round them. We looked out eagerly for water, but mile after mile was passed over and not a pool nor stream could we see. I suffered greatly from thirst, and sometimes thought that I should succumb. My uncle cheered me up, and Jan declared that we should soon reach water and be able to camp. Still on and on we went. At length Jan cried out—

"Dare water, dare water!"

I tried to lift up my head, but had not strength to move. I heard my uncle exclaim—

"A VAST HERD CAME SCAMPERING ACROSS THE PLAIN." [p. 40.

"Thank heaven! there's water, sure enough. I see the moonbeams playing on the surface of a pool."

I believe I fainted, for I remember no more until I found him splashing water over my face; and, opening my eyes. I saw him kneeling by my side. Jan was busily engaged in lighting a fire, while the ox was feeding not far off. A hut was then built for me, and as soon as I was placed in it I fell asleep. In the morning I awoke greatly revived. My uncle said he was determined to remain at the spot until I was sufficiently recovered to travel, and I promised to get well as soon as I could. When breakfast was over he started off with his gun to try and shoot a deer, for we had just exhausted the last remnant of venison we possessed.

As, sheltered from the rays of the sun, I lay in my hut, which was built on a slight elevation above the lakelet, I could enjoy a fine view of the country in front of me.

Jan, having just finished cleaning my gun, was engaged a little way below me in cutting up the wood for the fire, singing in a low voice one of his native songs.

Presently I caught sight of my uncle in the far distance advancing towards a rounded hillock which rose out of the plain below. Almost at the same moment, I saw still further off several animals which I at once knew to be deer coming on at a rapid rate towards our camp. They were taking a direction which would lead them close to where my uncle lay in ambush. They were followed by others in quick succession, until a vast herd came scampering and bounding across the plain like an army, two or three abreast, following each other. Twice I heard the report of my uncle's rifle. On each occasion a deer fell to the ground.

Jan cried out that they were blesboks, one of the finest deer in South Africa. They had long twisting horns, and were of a reddish colour, the legs being much darker, with a blaze of white on the face.

I never saw a more beautiful sight. Jan was all eagerness, and, taking my gun, he went in chase; but before he could get near enough to obtain a shot, the whole herd was scampering away across the plain, laughing at his puny efforts to overtake them.

In a short time my uncle appeared, carrying a portion of one of the animals on his back, and immediately sent off Jan with the ox to fetch in the remainder.

Here was wood and water, and game in abundance, so that we could not have chosen a better spot for remaining in until I was myself again. As we had plenty of meat he was able to concoct as much broth as I could consume. It contributed greatly to restore my strength; and, judging by the progress I was making, I hoped that we should be able shortly to resume our journey.

Chapter Three.

In a few days I was able to stroll a short distance from the camp, always taking my gun with me. Though I still walked with some difficulty, I every hour found my strength returning. Had we possessed a waggon we might have loaded it with skins, so abundant was the game; but, although we prepared a few of the most valuable, we could not venture to add much to the cargo of our poor ox. At last my uncle, seeing that I was strong enough to undertake the fatigue of the journey, announced his intention of setting off, and I determined that it should not be my fault if I broke down again.

In order to try my strength, I accompanied him on a short shooting excursion from the camp, where we left Jan to look after the ox and our goods. I found that I got along far better than I had expected; the satisfaction of once more finding myself able to move about greatly raising my spirits. We had gone but a short distance when looking over the bushes we saw some objects moving up and down which, as we crept nearer, turned out to be a pair of elephant's ears.

"We must have that fellow," said my uncle; "we

" ON WENT THE CREATURES, TRUMPETING WITH RAGE." [p. 46.

can carry his tusks, and one of his feet will afford us a substantial meal." The elephant, we fancied, did not see us; and keeping ourselves concealed by the underwood, we cautiously advanced. Presently we found ourselves on the borders of an open glade, a few low bushes only intervening between ourselves and the elephant. He now saw us clearly enough, and not liking our appearance, I suppose, lifted up his trunk and began trumpeting loudly.

"If he comes on, don't attempt to run," whispered my uncle, "but face him for a moment, and fire at his shoulder; then leap on one side or behind a tree, or if you can do so, climb up it with your rifle. I will look out for myself." As he spoke the elephant began to advance towards us. I fired, as did my uncle, the moment afterwards; but, though we both hit him, the huge beast, after approaching a few paces nearer, instead of charging, turned away to the left, and went crashing through the wood.

We having reloaded were about to follow him, when the heads of nearly a dozen other elephants appeared from the direction where we had seen the first; and, advancing rapidly through the shrubs which they trampled under foot, with trunks and tail stuck out, and uttering loud trumpetings, they came rushing like a torrent down upon us.

"Come behind these bushes!" cried my uncle, "and don't move thence if you value your life."

I felt as if my life was of very little value just then, for I could not see how we were to escape being crushed by the huge monsters as they rushed over us. My uncle fortunately possessed all the coolness required by an elephant hunter.

"Fire at that fellow opposite," he cried. "I'll take the next, and they'll probably turn aside."

We almost at the same moment pulled our triggers. The elephant at which my uncle fired stopped short, then down it came with a crash on its knees; while the one I aimed at rushed by with its companions, very nearly giving me an ugly kick with its feet.

We had both dropped behind the bush the moment we had delivered our fire. On went the creatures trumpeting with rage, and disappointed at not finding us.

We were not free from danger, for it was possible that they might return. As soon, therefore, as their tails had disappeared among the brushwood, we reloaded and ran towards some trees, the trunks of which would afford us some protection. Here we waited a short time in sight of the elephant which lay dead on the ground. We could hear the trumpeting of the others grow less distinct as they made their way through the forest, either influenced by fear or excited by rage, fancying they were still following us up.

"They will not come back for the present," said my uncle at length as

24

we issued out from among the trees, when he at once began to cut out the tusks from the dead elephant. These he calculated weighed together fully a hundred and ten pounds. This, however, was a greater weight than he could carry, and he would not allow me to attempt to help him.

"You shall convey one of the feet to the camp, and we will try our skill in cooking it," he said, dexterously cutting it off.

Taking a stick he ran it through the foot so that I could the more easily carry it. He then having shouldered one of the tusks, we set out for the camp, well satisfied with our day's sport.

As soon as we arrived we sent off Jan for the other tusk, as he could easily find the way by the track we had made; while my uncle dug a hole close to the fire, into which he raked a quantity of ashes, and then covered it up. After some time he again scraped out the ashes, and having wrapt the foot up in leaves, he put it into the hole, and covered it up with hot earth. On the top of all he once more lit a fire, and kept it blazing away for some time.

The fire had well-nigh burnt out when Jan returned with the other tusk. He told us that on his way back he had seen the spoors of the elephants, and that if we chose to follow them, he was sure that we should come up with them, and should most probably find those we had wounded.

We now uncovered our elephant's foot, which Jan pronounced to be as satisfactorily cooked as his own countrymen could have done it. The flesh was soft and gelatinous, greatly resembling calves-head, and was so tender that we could scoop it out with a spoon. I don't know that I ever enjoyed a meal more. Although we could not venture to load our ox with more than the two tusks we had already obtained, my uncle, hoping soon to fall in with Mr Welbourn, determined to try and obtain the tusks from the other two elephants we had wounded, and to leave them concealed, until we could send for them. There was the risk, of course, of their being discovered by the natives, as we were now approaching an inhabited part of the country. We had still a couple of hours of day-light, and as I did not feel myself fatigued with my previous exertions, my uncle agreed to allow me to accompany him, while Jan was left to clean the tusks and to prepare straps for carrying them on the back of the ox.

We soon discovered the elephants' spoor, and followed it for some distance, the splashes of blood we found here and there showing that the wounded animal had stopped to rest. It would be necessary, as we approached them, to be cautious, as they would be on the alert and ready to revenge themselves for the injury they had received.

We now every moment expected to come upon them. We stopped to listen; no sound could we hear to indicate that they were near us. We, therefore, went on until, reaching the top of a hillock, we caught sight of some water glittering among the trees. Advancing a little further a small lakelet opened out before us, in the shallow part of which, near the shore, stood an elephant, sucking up the water with his trunk and throwing it over his neck and shoulders.

My uncle remarked that he was sure it was the animal we had wounded, but that he was still too far off to give us a chance of killing him. We were making our way among the trees, hoping to got near without being perceived—though that was no easy matter as he kept his sharp eyes turning about in every direction—when, from behind the grove which had before concealed them, several more rushed out.

"They see us!" cried my uncle. "We must get up among the branches and shoot them as they pass, for they will not let us escape as easily as before."

Fortunately, near at hand was a tree, up which, without much difficulty, we could make our way. My uncle, going up first, helped me to follow him.

Scarcely had we secured ourselves when the elephants came up with their trunks sticking out and trumpeting as loudly as before. As they kept their eyes on the ground, they did not see us. We fired at them as they passed.

We remained for some time expecting the wounded elephant to follow its companions, but as it did not we began to hope that it had succumbed, and that we might find it dead in the neighbourhood. We were about to descend to look for it, when the heads of three giraffes, or camelopards, as they are sometimes called, appeared among the trees; the animals lifting up their tall necks to crop the leaves as they advanced. As they were coming in our direction we agreed to wait. By descending we might frighten them. In a short time one separated from the others, and got so close that my uncle could not resist the temptation of firing. As the shot entered its neck the graceful animal sank down to the ground, and lay perfectly dead. The other two trotted off to a short distance, alarmed by the report; but, seeing no human foe and not knowing what had happened to their companion, they stopped and continued browsing on the leaves as before.

"The chances are that they will soon come this way, and so we cannot do better than remain where we are," observed my uncle.

We sat some time watching the graceful creatures as they stretched up their long necks to a remarkable height, in search of the young shoots and leaves. Presently we saw one of them turn its head and look towards its dead companion. The next moment a lion burst out from among the bushes and sprang towards the giraffe on the ground. I had fancied that lions never condescended to feast on a dead animal; but probably there was still some little life in the giraffe, or, at all events, having only just been killed, the carcase could have had no savoury odour. Directly afterwards we heard a roar, and another lion sprang from the cover, the first replying with a roar which made the welkin ring. If we could not kill the lions, it was evident that we should soon have none of the meat to carry back with us. Instead, however, of beginning to tear the giraffe to pieces, the lions began walking round and round it and roaring lustily, possibly thinking that it was the bait to a trap, as they are taught by experience to be wary, many of their relatives having been caught in traps set by the natives. So occupied were the brutes with this matter that they did not discover us though we were at no great distance from them.

The two giraffes, on hearing the first lion roar, had trotted off, or they would probably have soon been attacked.

"Stay here, Fred!" whispered my uncle to me: "I will descend and get a shot at one of those fellows—don't be alarmed. If I kill him, the chances are the other runs off. At all events, I will retreat to the tree, and do you keep ready to fire, should he follow

me, while I reload. In the meantime there is no real danger."

I felt somewhat nervous at hearing this, though my uncle knew so well what he was about that I need not have been alarmed for his safety. Before I could reply he had descended the tree. Holding his rifle ready, he advanced towards the lions, but even then, as he was to leeward they did not discover him.

He was within fifteen paces of them, when he stopped and levelled his rifle. Just then they both saw him, and looked up as if greatly astonished at his audacity. He fired, and the first lion, giving a spring in the air, fell over on the body of the giraffe.

The second stopped, hesitating whether to leap on his enemy or to take to flight. This gave my uncle time to reload when he slowly stepped back towards the tree, facing the lion, which advanced at the same pace.

"Now, Fred! let me see what you can do," he shouted out as he found that the brute had got within range of my rifle.

I obeyed him, earnestly trusting that my shot would take effect. I felt sure that I had hit the animal, though, when the smoke cleared off, to my dismay I saw it about to spring at my uncle. He stood as calm as if the creature had been a harmless sheep. Just as the lion rose from the ground, I heard the crack of his rifle, and it fell back, shot through the heart. I quickly scrambled down to the ground to survey the giraffe and the two lions. My uncle seemed in no way elated by his victory. "If we had had our waggon we might have secured the skins," he observed; "but as it is, we must content ourselves with some of the giraffe's flesh, which we shall find palatable enough for want of better."

Drawing his knife, he at once commenced operations on the giraffe. We soon, having secured as much of the meat as we could require, ran a couple of sticks through it and started off to return to the camp.

Darkness, however, came down upon us before we had gone far; still, we hoped to be able to find our way. Scarcely, however, had the sun set, when the mutterings and roars of lions saluted our ears; and of course we had the uncomfortable feeling that at any moment one of them might spring out on us. We cast many an anxious glance round, and kept our rifles in our hands ready for instant use, hoping that we should have time to see a lion before he was upon us. We had no fear at present of human foes, as the country through which we were travelling was uninhabited; though we might fall in with hunting parties, who were, however, likely to prove friendly. Besides lions, there was a possibility of our encountering hyaenas, leopards, and wolves, which, when hunting in packs, are as dangerous as in other parts of the world.

My uncle made me go ahead, while he kept five or six paces behind, so that, should a lion spring out at me, he might be ready to come to my assistance. We kept shouting too, to scare away any of the brutes we most dreaded; for, savage as is the lion, he is a cowardly animal except when pressed by hunger. Fortunately the sky was clear, and the stars shining out brightly enabled us to steer our course by them; but we went on and on, and I began to fear that we had already passed our camp. I expressed my apprehensions to my uncle.

"No!" he answered, "we are all right. We shall see the fire in a short time, unless Jan has let it out, which is not likely."

"But perhaps a lion may have carried him off, and killed our ox also, and we shall then be in a sad plight," I remarked.

"Nonsense, Fred!" he answered; "you are overtired with your long walk, and allow gloomy apprehensions to oppress you. I wish that I had not brought you so far."

After this I said no more, but exerted myself to the utmost; though I could scarcely drag one foot after the other, and had it become necessary to run for our lives, I do not think I could have moved. I looked about, now on one side now on the other, and fancied that I could see the vast heads and shaggy manes of huge lions watching us from among the trees. I did not fear their roars as long as they were at a distance. At length I heard what I took to be the mutterings of half-a-dozen, at least, close to us. I shouted louder than ever, to try and drive them off. As soon as I stopped shouting I listened for my uncle's voice, dreading lest one of the brutes should have seized him. I could not stop, to look round, and I was most thankful when I again heard him shout—

"Go on, Fred; go on, my boy. We shall see Jan's camp-fire before long. I don't believe there's a lion within half a mile of us. During the night we hear their voices a long distance off."

At length I saw, right ahead, a glare cast on the trunks and branches of the trees. It was I hoped produced by our camp-fire. Again, again, we shouted; should any lions be stalking us, they were very likely to follow our footsteps close up to our camp, and might pounce down upon us at the last moment, fearful of losing their prey. I felt greatly relieved on hearing Jan's shout in reply to ours; and pushing eagerly on, we saw him sitting close to a blazing fire which he had made up. He was delighted to see us, for he had become very anxious at our long absence; especially as a troop of elephants, he said, had passed close to the camp; and, as one of them was wounded, he knew that they had been met with by us, and he feared might possibly have trampled us to death. He had heard, too, the roar of lions near at hand. We found the giraffe's flesh more palatable than I had expected. As soon as we had eaten a hearty supper we lay down to rest, Jan promising to remain awake and keep up a blazing fire so as to scare away the lions.

Every now and then I awoke, and could hear the roarings and mutterings of the monarchs of the forest, which I heartily wished were sovereigns of some other part of the world.

Greatly to my disappointment, after the fatigue I had gone through I was unable to travel the next morning, and we had to put off our departure for another day.

My uncle went out for a short time, to shoot an antelope or any other species of deer he could come across for provisions, as what he killed for food one day was unfit for eating the next.

He had been absent for some time, and as I felt that a short walk would do me good, I took my gun, intending not to go far from the camp. I had some hopes that I might come across an antelope or deer during my short excursion. I of course took good care to keep a look-out on either side, lest I should be surprised by a lion or a leopard, the animals mostly to be feared in that region. It was not impossible that I might fall in with an elephant, but I had no intention of attacking one if I did, and should have ample notice of its approach, so that I might keep out of its way. I had gone about a quarter of a mile or so from the camp, and was thinking of turning back when I reached a tree which I found I could easily climb, as the remains of branches stuck out almost close to the ground. I got up for the sake of taking a survey of the country around, and especially over that part of it we had to travel the next morning. I found my lofty seat very pleasant, for I was well shaded by the thick foliage over head, while a light breeze played among the leaves, which was refreshing in the extreme. I had some difficulty in keeping awake, but I endeavoured to do so fearful of letting go my gun, or, perhaps, of falling to the ground myself. I did my best not to fall asleep, by singing and by occasionally getting up and looking around me.

The tree grew, I should have said, on the side of a bank, with a wide extent of level ground to the eastward, dotted over with thick clumps of trees, some large enough to be called woods; while nearer at hand, on either side of me, the vegetation was more scattered, here and there two or three trees only growing together. In some places single trees alone could be seen, rising in solitary grandeur from the soil. I had just got up when I caught sight of an elephant, which had come out from one of the clumps I have mentioned, where it had probably been spending the hot hours of the day, and advanced slowly towards me, now plucking a bunch of leaves with its trunk, now pulling up a shrub or plant. Presently I caught sight of a man with a gun in his hand coming out from the forest to the left and making his way towards where the elephant was feeding. He apparently did not see the animal, which was hidden from him by an intervening clump. When he got closer I recognised my uncle. Wishing to warn him of the neighbourhood of the elephant, I shouted as loudly as I could bawl; but, from the distance we were apart, he could not hear me. The elephant also took no notice of my voice, but went on feeding as before.

Presently my uncle came in sight of the monstrous beast, which must have seen him at the same time, for it ceased feeding and turned its head in the direction he was coming. Nothing daunted, my uncle continued to advance, keeping, however, more to the right, which would bring him towards the tree on which I was perched. The elephant began to move towards him. He quickened his pace—he was now in the open ground, over which he was making his way, exposed to great danger. He was aware of this and kept his gun ready to fire, though should he miss, he would be at the mercy of the brute. I

"THE ELEPHANT, ELEVATING ITS TRUNK, ACTUALLY TOUCHED HIS FOOT." [p. 61.

considered how I could help him, but saw it would be madness to descend the tree to fire, and therefore remained where I was, praying that, should my uncle fire, his shot might be successful.

Presently, up went the elephant's trunk; and, trumpeting loudly, he went at a fast trot directly towards my uncle, who, stopping for a moment, levelled his rifle and fired; but, although the shot took effect, it did not stop the elephant's progress.

He had not a moment to reload—flight was his only resource. Happily not far off was a tree, but whether its branches grew low down enough to enable him to climb up it, I could not see, and I trembled for his safety. I shouted and shrieked, hoping to divert the attention of the elephant. It appeared to me that its trunk was not a dozen yards from my uncle. Should it once encircle him, his fate would be sealed. I never felt more anxious in my life. I might still stop its course I hoped, and, raising my rifle, I fired at its head, but my bullet seemed to make not the slightest impression. I shrieked with alarm. The next moment I saw my uncle seize the bough of a tree which had appeared to me above his head, when, exerting all his strength, he drew himself up. The elephant, elevating its trunk, actually touched his foot, but he drew it beyond its reach, and quickly clambered up into a place of safety. The elephant stood for a moment, its trunk raised as if expecting him to fall, and then made a furious dash at the tree in a vain endeavour to batter it down. The tree trembled from the shock but stood firm.

The elephant then, taking my uncle's cap which had fallen off, trampled it under foot, going round and round the tree and trumpeting loudly. It was evidently a rogue elephant, an ill-tempered brute who had been driven from the herd to spend a solitary existence. Such are always the most dangerous, as they appear to have a greater hatred of man and to be more cunning than the elephants found in herds. It seemed to have made up its mind to besiege us. Our position was unpleasant in the extreme, for while it remained we dared not descend, and for what we could tell, we might be kept up our respective trees all night, and perhaps the following day, or still longer.

Chapter Four.

My uncle and I felt far from happy up our trees. He had had nothing to eat since he left camp in the morning, and I too was getting *very* hungry. An hour or more went by, and yet the old "rogue" elephant showed no inclination to take its departure. Fortunately it had not discovered my uncle's rifle, which lay concealed in the grass close to the foot of the tree.

He now shouted to me to try to shoot the brute. This was no easy matter perched as I was high up; and as I was not likely to hit any vital part, I feared that any shot would only contribute to increase its rage without bringing it to the ground or driving it off. I had but five more bullets in my pouch, but I determined to do my best and not throw a shot away. I waited until the animal presented its side to me, when I fired, and the bullet struck it on the neck; but, though the blood flowed, it seemed to take no notice of the wound. The next I planted just below the shoulder. The elephant uttered several loud trumpetings and rushing again at the tree, seized the stem with its trunk, and endeavoured to pull it down. It shook violently, compelling my uncle to hold on with arms and legs.

I quickly reloaded and fired another shot directly behind the creature's ear. I saw the blood spouting forth and flowing down until it formed a pool dyeing the surrounding grass. Gradually the elephant's trunk unwound and hung down from its vast head.

"You've done for it," shouted my uncle; "send another shot into its neck and we shall be free."

I was reloading while he spoke, and before the elephant altered its favourable position I again fired.

Less than a minute elapsed, then down it sank on its knees. It made several efforts to rise but without success—its strength was fast failing. I had one more bullet remaining, but I wished to save it for any emergency which might occur. We had not long to wait before the elephant fell over on its side and lay an inanimate mass.

My uncle quickly descended the tree and I followed his example. His first act was to pick up and examine his gun. It having escaped injury he at once reloaded, and then, shaking hands, we surveyed our fallen foe.

"I wish that we could carry these magnificent tusks with us, but that is

34

out of the question," observed my uncle. "We will, however, try to secure them. Help me to cut them out."

We set to work; and having fastened all the straps we could muster round one of them, he ascended the tree in which I had taken refuge, and I assisting him, we hauled up one of the tusks, and deposited it safely among the branches. The other was hauled up in the same fashion, and pretty hard work it was, as each tusk was considerably above half a hundredweight.

"I hope that we shall be able to send for these some day or other, and we are not likely to forget this spot in a hurry," remarked my uncle.

Having cut off one of the elephant's feet we ran a stick through it and started off for the camp. The day, however, was not to pass without another adventure. We had not gone half the distance when we saw, above the bushes, the head and neck of a giraffe. It did not appear to be alarmed; but influenced by curiosity, instead of cantering away, it drew nearer, coming round the end of the clump, evidently wondering what strange creatures we could be. So interested was it that it did not notice another and more formidable enemy which had been creeping up close behind. This was a lion, which, engaged in stalking its prey, did not discover us. We, therefore, could watch at a safe distance what was taking place. The lion kept creeping on, cautious as a cat, and with movements very similar, when, believing that it had got near enough for its purpose, with a rush and a tremendous bound, it leapt on the back of the giraffe before the latter could use its heels to drive off its foe. With fearful tenacity the savage creature hung on to the shoulders of the terrified giraffe, which bounded forward, and leapt and sprang from side to side in a vain endeavour to shake off its foe. Not a sound did it utter, but dashed on, with head erect; while the lion was tearing away with its teeth and claws at its shoulders and neck. There was no doubt from the first which of the two would gain the victory. Blood was streaming from the neck and flanks of the poor giraffe, which very quickly slackened its pace and then down it came, unable longer to endure the pain it was suffering. The lion at once began tearing away at the flesh. Still it kicked, and struggled, but its efforts were useless, and it very quickly ceased to move.

"We must have that lion," said my uncle.

Having examined our rifles we hurried towards the spot where the savage brute was enjoying its banquet, so busily employed that it did not see us. When at length it was aware of our approach it ceased feeding, and gazed at us with its fore paws on the body of its victim, presenting a truly magnificent spectacle.

We were near enough by this time to take a steady aim.

"Do you fire, Fred, and then reload as rapidly as you can, while I will wait until you are ready."

"But I have no second bullet," fortunately recollecting at the moment that I had expended all my bullets but one.

My uncle handed me a couple, and I obeyed his injunctions. My bullet passed through the lion's thick mane and crashed into its neck.

Uttering a tremendous roar as it felt the pain, it came towards us. Without a moment's loss of time I reloaded, fearing that, should my uncle's bullet fail to stop it, the brute would be upon us.

Notwithstanding the lion's near approach my uncle waited, and then fired, hitting it between the eyes. Still it advanced, but, blinded and almost stunned, though it made a desperate bound towards us, its aim was uncertain. My uncle sprang on one side and I

"WITH A RUSH IT LEAPT ON THE BACK OF THE GIRAFFE."
[p. 65.

on the other, when, before I had finished loading, over it fell, and lay dead between us.

"A pretty good afternoon's sport," observed my uncle. "We'll take the liberty of cutting a few steaks from the giraffe which this brute here has hunted for us, and the sooner we get back to camp the better."

The chief difficulty in obtaining the steaks was in cutting through the tough skin of the giraffe, which was almost as thick as that of a rhinoceros. By employing our axes we soon, however, accomplished our task, and in a few minutes reached the camp, where Jan, who had heard our shots, had made up a large fire in expectation of any game we should bring.

While the elephant foot was cooking we regaled ourselves on some fine slices of giraffe meat, which assisted to stop the cravings of hunger. All night long we were surrounded by the abominable cries of hyaenas and jackals which were collected round the carcases of the slain animals.

It is said that they dare not touch even a dead lion, but at all events when we went out to look the next morning the bones only of the two animals remained.

We now once more reloaded our ox and set out northward. We remarked that the poor creature, in spite of its long rest, looked thinner, and in worse condition than before.

"Him tsetse do it. You see, ox die!" exclaimed Jan.

Still the faithful brute stepped on with its heavy load, and we hoped that Jan was mistaken.

At length we came in sight of a broader river than we had crossed since we had left the desert.

We had no doubt that it would conduct us down to the lake, on the borders of which we hoped to find our friends encamped. How to cross it was the difficulty. I suggested that we should construct a raft, as the reeds which fringed the bank would supply us with abundance of material.

Not far off was a tree-covered island, the intervening space being filled with reeds. Leaving Jan and the ox on the shore, my uncle and I set off to reach the island, thinking that we could there more conveniently build our raft and launch it than from the main land.

Plunging in among the reeds we soon found ourselves almost overwhelmed: not a breath of air could reach us, and the heat was so stifling that we almost fainted. Still, having begun, we were unwilling to give up.

Frequently we could only get on by leaning against the mass of reeds, and bending them down until we could stand upon them. They were mixed with a serrated grass which cut our hands, while the whole was bound together by the climbing convolvulus, with stalks so strong that we could not break them.

Plying our axes, however, we managed to make our onward way until we gained the island, but here to our disappointment we found that we were thirty yards or more from the clear water, which was full of great masses of papyrus with stalks ten feet in height, and an inch and a half in diameter. These also were bound together by the convolvulus in a

way which

"SUDDENLY, DOWN CAME THE HARPOON."   [A 72.

made them perfectly impenetrable. While we stood on the shore of the island the sound of human voices reached our ears, and we saw in the distance several canoes descending the stream. Each carried three men, two paddling and one standing up with a large harpoon attached to a rope in his hand. They were in pursuit of some large dark creatures whose heads, just rising above the water, looked like those of enormous cart-horses.

"They are hippopotami!" exclaimed my uncle, "and we shall see some sport presently."

Suddenly, down came the harpoon, and was fixed in the back of one of the monsters, which almost sprang out of the water as it felt the pain of the wound; then off it went, towing the canoe at a tremendous rate after it, the end of the rope being secured to the bows, while the barb to which the rope was attached being shaken out of its socket remained firmly fixed in the animal's body.

We ran along the island to watch the canoe as long as it remained in sight, but it was towed so rapidly that it soon disappeared. Presently,

38

however, we saw another coming down the stream fast to a second hippopotamus, not only the head but a considerable portion of the body of which was floating above the water. The men in the canoe were hauling themselves up closer to their prey, preparatory to plunging their lances or harpoons into its body. I fancied that I could almost distinguish the savage glance of the brute's eyes. Suddenly it stopped; then, turning round, gave a rush at the canoe.

In vain the blacks slackened the rope, and seizing

"THEN OFF IT WENT, TOWING THE CANOE AT A TREMENDOUS RATE AFTER IT." [A. 72.

their paddles, endeavoured to escape from it. With open mouth the hippopotamus rushed on the boat, and, seizing it in its enormous jaws, crushed it up as if it had been made of paper.

One poor fellow was caught; a fearful shriek was heard; and, directly afterwards, we saw his body, cut in two, floating down the stream. The other two men had disappeared, and we fancied must also have been killed. Again and again the animal darted at the canoe, expending his rage upon it.

While he was thus employed the two men rose to the surface and instantly made for the shore, dragging the end of the rope by a path we had not before observed, between the reeds. With wonderful activity they made it fast to the trunk of a tree. Directly afterwards three other canoes arrived, and the men, armed with harpoons and heavy spears, jumping on shore, joined their companions in hauling in on the rope attached to the hippopotamus. In vain the monster struggled, endeavouring to tear itself away from the rope. The blacks with wonderful boldness rushed into the water, darting their spears at it. It had seized the shaft of the harpoon, which had broken in two, and was endeavouring to bite through the rope.

Two other canoes now came up and their crews attacked the hippopotamus in the rear. So engaged were the hunters that they did not observe us. As we watched their proceedings it appeared very probable that in spite of its wounds the hippopotamus would break away. Seeing this, my uncle unslung his rifle and advanced towards the monster, which had already severed several strands of the rope. As it opened its vast mouth, he fired down its throat, and it almost instantly, giving another convulsive struggle, rolled over.

His success was greeted with triumphant shouts by the hunters who had only just before discovered us. Having drawn the body of the hippopotamus up to the dry land, the blacks crowded round us, and by signs and exclamations expressed their admiration of the way in which my uncle had killed the creature.

We tried to explain that we were very happy to have been of service to them, and that we should feel obliged, if, in return, they would ferry us across the river, and guide us to the waggons of the white men who had encamped not far off.

Leaving the hunters to cut up the hippopotamus, and stow its flesh on board their canoes, we returned to where we had left Jan and the ox. As it was getting late, we agreed to remain where we were until the following day,—in the meantime to try to shoot an antelope or deer of some sort which would enable us to provide a feast for the natives by whom we might be visited.

I was fortunate enough, while lying down among some rocks near our camp, to kill a springbok, one of the most light and elegant of the gazelle tribe; but its companions, of which it had several, bounded off at so rapid a rate that I had no chance of killing another. I, therefore, lifting my prize on my shoulder, returned to camp, where my uncle soon after arrived, laden with the flesh of a quagga, which, although belonging to the family of asses, is good food.

Scarcely had we put on some meat to cook, when half a dozen of our acquaintances arrived. It was satisfactory to find that Jan understood their language. They appeared to be well-disposed towards us, and our friendship was cemented by the feast of quagga flesh which we got ready for them. We ourselves, however, preferred the more delicate meat of the springbok. We kept some of the meat for our next day's breakfast, and offered the remainder to our guests, which they quickly stowed away.

They undertook to convey us down the river the following morning in their canoes, or on a raft, observing that, if we went in the canoes, we must be separated, as each could carry only one of us. We, therefore, determined to trust to a raft, such as we ourselves had proposed

40

building. Our guests retired for a short distance from us, and formed a camp by themselves for the night.

I awoke about two hours before dawn, when my attention was attracted to a peculiar noise which I might liken to a low grunting and the tread of numberless feet. As day broke, I saw the ground to the southward covered with a dense mass of deer moving slowly and steadily on towards an opening in a long range of hills to the east. They appeared to be in no hurry, but continued feeding as they went. I aroused my uncle, who pronounced them to be springboks, one of which I had shot on the previous evening migrating for the winter to the northward. They were beautiful animals, graceful in form, of a light cinnamon red on the back, fading into white on the under part of the body, a narrow band of reddish brown

"THE BLACKS RUSHED INTO THE WATER, DARTING THEIR SPEARS AT IT." [p. 74.

separating the two colours. As far as the eye could reach, the whole country seemed alive with them,—not only the plain but the hill-side, along which they bounded with graceful leaps.

Our guests on the previous evening had disappeared, but they quickly came back with a large party of their tribe, and gave us to understand that they could not escort us down to the river for the present, as they must set out to attack the springboks, and hoped that we would accompany them.

This my uncle and I at once agreed to do, and, supplying ourselves with a good stock of ammunition, we set off with the first party that started. Our friends led us at a rapid rate over the hills by a short cut, so that we might intercept the animals, as they passed through the mountains. Another party, we found, remained behind, to drive them through, or prevent them turning back when frightened by our

41

presence. We were only just in time, for already the leaders of the herd had made their appearance. As we approached the mouth of the gorge, while some of the hunters rushed up the hills, and stationed themselves on either side, so as to dart their javelins at the passing deer, others took post at the mouth of the gorge, thus preventing the egress of the animals, without coming within range of their weapons.

Now a scene of slaughter commenced such as I have seldom witnessed. The leaders of the herd turned to retreat, but were met by the party who had remained on the other side shrieking and shouting, and knocking the handles of their spears against their shields. Some of the animals tried to escape up the mountains, others dashed forward to our very feet, and many fell down killed by terror itself. We shot a few, but the slaughter seemed so unnecessary that we refrained from again firing, and would gladly have asked the natives to desist; but while the animals were in their power, they would evidently have refused to do so.

Happily the affrighted deer found an opening, which, from the excessive steepness of the path, had been neglected. Through this a considerable number made their escape, and were soon beyond the reach of their merciless pursuers.

The natives now began to collect the animals they had slain, and each man returned in triumph with a springbok on his shoulders.

We, not to be outdone, each carried one of those we had shot, and a pretty heavy load it was. I was thankful when we got back to the camp, where we cooked a portion of the venison.

As we might have felt sure, the natives, having plenty of food, were not at all disposed to move from the spot, and, indeed, continued feasting the whole of the next day. On the following, they were so gorged that they were utterly unable to make any exertion. Had an enemy been near, and found them in this condition, the whole tribe might have been killed or carried off into captivity.

We in the meantime explored the banks of the river until we found a convenient spot for forming our raft. In most places the reeds extended so far from the shore that during the operation we should have had to stand up to our middles in water among them,

"NOW A SCENE OF SLAUGHTER COMMENCED." *p. 79.* with the risk of being picked up by a crocodile or hippopotamus, both of which delectable creatures were, in considerable numbers, frequenters of the stream.

As the blacks still showed no inclination to accompany us, Jan volunteered to return for the elephant's tusks and other articles we had left behind, if I would go with him.

To this my uncle somewhat demurred, but, at last, when I pressed the point, he consented to remain in charge of the goods we had brought while we set off on our expedition.

Chapter Five.

At daybreak Jan and I set off, he as usual leading the ox, while I walked ahead with my rifle, ready for a shot. Our baggage consisted of a couple of skins to sleep on, a stock of ammunition, a small portion of our remnant of flour, tea, sugar, and pepper. We had no fear of not finding food, as game of all sorts was abundant, provided I kept my health, and was able to shoot it.

I asked Jan what he thought of the ox which looked remarkably thin.

"No good!" he answered; "last till get back, but not more—den him die."

I trusted that the poor animal would hold out as long as he supposed.

We rested at noon under an enormous acacia, of the younger

43

branches of which the elephants are apparently very fond. We saw that they were everywhere twisted off to the height of about twenty-five feet, which is as far as an elephant can reach.

Here and there, under the trees, were conical hills twenty feet high, built up for residences by the white ants. Frequently they were covered with creeping plants which met at the top, hanging back in an umbrella shape, completely shading them. I shot several doves and other birds to serve us for dinner, and while Jan was cooking them I went in search of fruit, and discovered an abundance of medlars very similar to those we have in England, as well as some small purple figs growing on bushes. The most curious fruit I met with was like a lime in appearance, with a thick rind, but inside was a large nut. I had to climb a tree to obtain them, for all those lower down had been carried off by elephants who were evidently very fond of the fruit.

As our object was to make as much haste as possible, I was resolved not to go out of the way to shoot any large game, though I kept my rifle loaded with ball as a defence against lions, leopards, rhinoceroses, or hyaenas.

The first day's journey we saw several in the distance, though none came near us. We formed our camp at the foot of a tree, with a large fire in front of us, and on either side of the trunk we erected a fence of stout stakes in a semi-circular form; so we hoped that we should be able to sleep without being molested by wild beasts. The ox remained outside, and we knew that he would run to the fire, should danger threaten him.

The usual cries proceeding from an African forest prevented us from sleeping over soundly, and I was awakened by the roar of a lion, which stood on a mound some little distance from our camp, afraid of approaching near our fire, and the palisade which he probably took for a trap.

We had exhausted our stock of wood during the night, and in the morning Jan went out to procure a fresh supply for cooking our breakfast. I was employed in plucking some birds which I had killed in the evening, when I heard my companion shouting lustily for help, and at the same time, a loud crashing of boughs reached my ears, while the ox came hurrying up to the camp in evident alarm.

Seizing my rifle, I sprang up, fearing that a lion had pounced down upon Jan, while picking up sticks, and I was fully prepared for an encounter with the savage brute. Instead of a lion, however, I saw an elephant, with trunk uplifted, rush out from among the brushwood. I sprang behind a tree, as the only place of safety, when what was my dismay, to see, as he passed, Jan clinging to his hind leg. How the black had got there was the puzzle, and how to rescue him from his awkward position was the next question to be solved. Should he let go, he might naturally expect to receive a kick from the elephant's hind foot which would effectually knock all the breath out of his body; and yet, should he not get free, he might be carried miles away and perish miserably. My only hope was at once to mortally wound the elephant. Not a moment was to be lost if I was to save poor Jan. Just then the elephant caught sight of the ox, and stopped as if considering if he should attack it. Whether he was aware that Jan was clinging to his leg or not, I could not tell, as the black's weight no more impeded him than a fly would a man when running.

The ox, instead of endeavouring to escape, presented its head to the elephant, though it trembled in every limb.

45

Jan, who seemed paralysed with fear, did not let go as I thought he would have done, and his best chance would have been to spring back, even though he had fallen on the ground directly behind the elephant. I did not like to shout to him for fear of attracting the creature's attention.

Now or never was my time to save the poor fellow. I stepped from under cover of the tree, and, levelling my rifle, aimed at a spot directly behind the ear.

The huge monster did not move, then presently it began swaying to and fro. I shouted to Jan to leap off and hurried on to help him. Before I reached the spot, he had followed my advice, and hardly had he done so, than down came the elephant with a crash, to the ground. Jan raised a shout of triumph.

"De master hab done well!" he cried out. I could not help joining him, and even the ox gave a bellow of satisfaction as he saw his huge foe stretched lifeless on the ground.

We at once set to work to extract the tusks with our axes. Rather than leave them, we agreed to take them with us. We therefore placed them on the back of our ox, together with some slices of elephant meat which would prevent the necessity of shooting game during the day.

We now pushed forward for the cave where we had left our goods, and met with no adventures worth noticing. We saw numerous herds of antelopes, giraffes, and a few ostriches. The latter I would have killed if I could, for the sake of their valuable feathers. The cave had been untouched, and it was with no small satisfaction that I loaded up the ox with its contents, as we prepared to set off the next morning on our return, intending, on our way back, to obtain the elephant's tusks we had deposited in the tree, which had afforded me such seasonable shelter when attacked by their owner.

We met as before buffaloes, elands, koodoos, and various antelopes. As I was walking along ahead, suddenly I found my face enveloped as if by a thick veil; and as I was tearing off the web—for such it was—I caught sight of a large yellow spider, hauling himself up to the tree above. In the neighbourhood were many other webs, the fibres radiating from a centre point where the greedy insect was waiting for its prey.

Each web was about a yard in diameter, and the lines on which they were hung, suspended from one tree to another, were as thick as coarse thread. We occasionally met with serpents, but they generally kept out of our way.

One day, during a halt, while seated under a tree, I caught sight of another enormous spider of a reddish tinge. Never did I see a creature so active. It suddenly made its appearance from a hole in the bark, and giving a tremendous bound, caught a large moth which it quickly devoured. With wonderful rapidity it ran about the tree, now darting forward, now springing back. With a feeling of horror lest it should spring upon me, I removed to a distance. On looking down on the ground, I saw what I at first thought was a coin the size of a shilling; but on looking closer I discovered that it was of a pure white silky substance like paper, and that it formed the door to a hole. On trying to lift it up I discovered that it was fastened by a hinge on one side, and on turning it over upon the hole it fitted exactly—the upper side being covered with earth and grass, so that, had it not been for the circumstance that the inmate had been out, I could not possibly have detected it. Jan said it was the hole of a spider, probably the creature I had seen engaged in seeking its prey.

While encamped that night, I heard the crashing of heads and horns. Jan told me it was caused by a troop of buffaloes who were fighting. Presently a loud snorting and puffing reached our ears. The uproar increased, and he declared that the noise was produced by rhinoceroses and buffaloes quarrelling. My fear was that in their heady fight the animals might come our way and trample over us, or perhaps the rhinoceroses would attack our poor ox, who was but ill able to defend himself.

While I was looking out beyond our camp-fire I caught sight of a herd of elephants, the huge males going first, followed by the females, on their way down to a large pool where they were going to drink. I followed them cautiously until they entered the water.

Having satisfied their thirst, they began throwing it over themselves and disporting in the cool element, gambolling and rolling about like a party of schoolboys bathing. As I could not have carried away their tusks, I did not attempt to shoot one but left

"; FIRED AT ITS HEAD."   [p. 94 them unmolested. After a while I saw them returning by the way they had come, appearing in the uncertain light like huge phantoms so noiselessly did they stalk over the ground.

It is strange that, huge as the elephant is, from the soft padding of its feet, the sound of its steps is not heard even on hard ground. Its approach is only to be discovered by the snapping of boughs and twigs as it makes its way among the brushwood.

We were but a short distance from the spot where we had left the elephant's tusks, one of the objects of our expedition. I felt very sure of the place, as the adventure we had there met with had marked it in my memory.

I was going up to the tree followed by Jan, when I saw an object moving among the branches. This made me approach cautiously, and fortunately I did so, for on looking up, I caught sight of an enormous leopard, which probably had been attracted by the smell of the flesh still adhering to the roots of the tusks. As the creature had got possession of the tree, I had first to dislodge him before I could obtain our tusks; that they were still there I discovered by seeing their points sticking out beyond the forks of the boughs where we had deposited them. I knew the leopard's habit of leaping down on passing animals, and thought it might attempt to catch me in the same manner. I therefore stood at a distance, but though I shouted at the top of my voice, and threw pieces of wood at it, it held its post, snarling and growling savagely.

"Better shoot him, or he come down when no tinkee," cried Jan, who had remained with the ox at a safe distance.

As we were in a hurry to move on, I saw that the sooner I did this the better, but it was important to shoot it dead, for should I miss or only wound it, it might make its leap before I had reloaded, and attack me and Jan.

I advanced, and taking good aim, pulled the trigger, but what was my dismay to find my gun miss fire, while at the same moment the leopard made a spring from a high bough on which it was perched. I expected the next instant to feel its fangs in my neck, and be struck to the ground by its sharp claws; but happily its feet caught in some of the creeping vines which were entwined round the tree, and it very nearly came toppling to the ground on its head. Recovering itself, however, it pitched on a lower bough.

I, in the meantime, endeavouring to be calm, cleaned out the nipple of my gun, and put a fresh cap on; then retiring a few paces while the creature gazed down upon me, about to make another spring, I fired at its head, into which the bullet buried itself, and down it crashed to the ground.

I leaped back, and reloading, stood ready to give it another shot, but this was unnecessary; after a few convulsive struggles, it lay helpless on the ground. On drawing near I found that it was dead. The skin being a handsome one, I determined to secure it. With Jan's assistance, I soon had it off and placed on the back of the ox. I now ascended the tree, and found that though the ends of the tusks were gnawed, they were not otherwise injured.

With the aid of Jan I lowered them down, and secured them to the back of the ox. The poor brute was now overloaded, but as we had not far to go, I hoped that it would be able to carry its burden that short distance.

Had I been strong I would have endeavoured to carry some of the load, but I found my gun and ammunition, with the birds I occasionally shot, quite enough for me. At length, greatly to my satisfaction, we drew near the spot where I had left my uncle on some high ground overlooking the river. Every moment I thought that our poor ox would give in.

We might, I suspect, have been indicted by the Society for the Prevention of Cruelty to Animals, had we been seen urging on the ox, but we had no choice, for had we abandoned our goods, the natives would have taken possession of them. At last, as evening was approaching, we caught sight of my uncle's camp-fire. We shouted, as he did in return, when he came hurrying down the hill to meet us.

"What poor brute have you got there?" he exclaimed, after welcoming us.

When I told him it was our old ox, he would scarcely believe it to be the same animal. Hardly was the burden off its back, and Jan was about to lead it down to the water, than the poor creature, giving a convulsive shudder, fell to the ground, and in a few minutes was dead, having faithfully performed its duty to the last. I felt more sad than I could have supposed it possible, as I assisted my uncle and Jan in drawing away the carcase from the camp. We had not dragged it far, before some natives arrived, who relieved us of all further trouble, saying that they would take it to their camp, and eat it in spite of its having died from the effects of the tsetse poison, which we warned them was the case.

My uncle told me that he had prepared a raft, which would convey us and our goods down the river to where Mr Welbourn's camp was situated, and that he had engaged a couple of canoes and a party of natives to accompany us. Instead of the howling of wild beasts, we were serenaded during the night by the shouts of laughter and songs of the blacks feasting on the carcase of the poor ox. It was quite as well, however, that it should be eaten by them, as by jackals, which would have been its fate had it died in the wilderness.

Next morning, assisted by the blacks, we carried our goods down to the river, where we found a curious raft constructed of reeds. It appeared to me loosely thrown together, somewhat like the top of a floating haystack. My uncle said that the natives had formed it by throwing on the calm water a number of reeds, which were interlaced together. Then others were added, until the lower sank by the weight of those pressed upon them, it being built up until it rose to a sufficient height above the surface to bear as many men and as much cargo as it was required to carry. In the centre was stuck a mast to which a sail made of skins, was twisted, while a long oar projecting astern served to guide it. Notwithstanding the assurances of the natives that it was fit to perform a long voyage, I was glad of the attendance of the canoes.

All things being ready, amid the shouts of the people on shore, we shoved off, and, being towed cut into the stream by the canoes, set sail. Considering the clumsy nature of our raft, we glided on with great rapidity, the canoemen having to paddle pretty hard to keep up with us.

It was pleasant to be reclining at our ease, and to be borne along without having to exert ourselves. The voyage, however, was not without its dangers. Now and then a huge hippopotamus would show its ugly head alongside, threatening to overturn our frail craft, which it might easily have done with one heave of its back. Occasionally, too, crocodiles would swim by, looking up at us with their savage eyes, showing us how we should be treated should we by any chance be sent splashing into the water. About mid-day we steered for the shore where our black crew intimated that they intended to dine.

The raft was secured by a rope round the mast and carried to the trunk of a tree. We, however, were unwilling to leave our goods on board without a guard, and therefore determined to remain where we were and to eat a cold meal; the materials for which we had brought with us. The water appearing bright and tempting, I was about to plunge overboard, when I felt the raft give a heave. Directly afterwards, a huge crocodile poked his ugly snout above the surface, warning me that I had better remain where I was. Two or three others made their appearance soon afterwards in the neighbourhood. My uncle and I agreed that the sooner we were away from the spot the better, as any of the savage brutes coming under the raft might upset it, and we should be committed to their tender mercies.

We were very glad, therefore, when the blacks, having finished their meal, returned on board, and we once more began to float down the stream.

We were in hopes that at the rate we were proceeding we should meet our friends before the close of the day, but darkness approached, and the blacks gave us to understand that we must go on shore and spend the night at a village of their tribe, where we should be hospitably entertained. To this we could offer no objection, though it involved the necessity of landing our goods, as we had no fancy to spend the time on the raft, with the prospect of finding it melting away below our feet, and we ourselves left to be devoured by the crocodiles, or perhaps, to have it capsized by the heave of an hippopotamus beneath it.

51

As we glided on, we saw a collection of bee-hive looking huts on the top of the south bank. The raft was directed towards them. The natives, leaping on shore, secured it as before by a rope to a tree growing on the beach. They then assisted in carrying our property to the shore. Having piled it up in a heap and covered it over with a roof of leaves, they assured us that it would be as safe as if guarded by a hundred men. As they had hitherto shown themselves to be scrupulously honest, we had no reason to doubt them on this occasion; and we, therefore, willingly accompanied them to the village, whence a number of people issued forth to greet us. They then conducted us to a newly built hut, the inside of which was as clean as we could desire, the floor covered with freshly made mats. There we could more securely rest than we had been able to do for a long time. We were, however, not yet allowed to enter it; a feast was preparing at which it was expected we should be present, after which there was to be a dance for our entertainment. For the feast a fat ox had been killed, part being roasted and part stewed. Some of both was placed before us, together with huge bowls of porridge, which our entertainers mixed with their fingers, and transferred by the same means to their mouths in large quantities. They looked somewhat surprised when we hesitated to follow their example, but considering that it would show mistrust, we at last overcame our repugnance. The porridge itself was certainly not bad, and our hosts laughed heartily as they saw how we burnt our fingers and made wry faces. The whole was washed down with huge draughts of pombe, a sort of beer, with slightly intoxicating properties. We did not inquire too minutely as to how it was made. The feast over, we heard an extraordinary uproar proceeding from another part of the village, a sound between the barking of dogs and people endeavouring to clear their throats. On going in the direction whence the strange sounds came, we found several men with spears in their hands and anklets of shells fastened round their legs, bending over a small fire, and producing the melancholy noises which had attracted our attention. Others danced round them rattling their anklets, while a party of women forming an outer semicircle sang a monotonous chant and clapped their hands. The old men and women, the senior inhabitants of the village, whom we were invited to join, sat on the opposite side, spectators of the performance. In the meantime the young men and boys were prancing about, now advancing to the girls beating the ground, rattling their anklets, and creating an enormous quantity of dust.

These proceedings had gone on for some time, when a gay youth, evidently the leader among them, snatching a brand from the fire after dancing up to the girls, stuck it in the ground, when he began to leap round and over it, for a considerable time, taking care not to touch it.

After these various scenes had been enacted, a number of young men, representing a war party returning victorious from battle, made their appearance, and brandishing their broad-headed spears, ornamented with flowing ox-tails. Now they rushed off, as if to pursue an enemy; now returned, and were welcomed by a chorus from the women.

The scene was highly effective; the glare of the fire being reflected on the red helmet-like gear and glittering ornaments of the girls, on the flashing blades and waving ox-tails on the warriors, and the figures of the spectators, with the huts and groups of cattle in the distance, while the howling, chanting, shrieking, and barking sounds were kept up without intermission. We, at last, making signs to the chief

"A PARTY OF WOMEN SANG A MONOTONOUS CHANT AND CLAPPED THEIR HANDS."

that we were very weary, placing our heads on our hands and closing our eyes, were led ceremoniously to our hut, into which we were thankful to enter. Having closed the entrance we lay down and tried to go to sleep. The noises which reached our ears showed us, however, that the dance was being kept up with unabated spirit, and I suspect that our hosts formed but a mean opinion of our tastes in consequence of our disappearing from the festive scene.

Next morning, having bestowed a few remaining trinkets to delight the hearts of the black damsels, we wished our hospitable entertainers farewell and continued our voyage, not an article of our property having been purloined.

Our raft clung together far better than I should have supposed, but I suspect, had it struck a rocky bottom, the case would have been very different. We passed by herds of hippopotami, some with young ones on their backs, and although they sank as we approached, they soon came to the surface to breathe. On the trees overhead were numbers of iguanas, which, on seeing us, splashed into the water. The chief canoeman carried a light javelin, with which he speared a couple, the flesh proving to be tender and gelatinous.

Numerous large crocodiles, as we appeared, plunged heavily into the stream, indeed there was everywhere an abundance of animal life. Had we not been anxious to join our friends, we should have been contented to continue the voyage for several days longer.

Another evening was approaching when we espied beneath a huge tree what looked like a tent and a couple of waggons near it. We fired off our guns as a signal, and in a short time we saw two white men coming towards us. We quickly landed in one of the canoes, and were soon shaking hands with Mr Welbourn and his son Harry.

Chapter Six.

Mr Welbourn had a good stock of ammunition, and with the supply we brought it was considered that we had sufficient to enable us to continue the journey northward into a region where elephants abounded. The cattle were in good condition, and, provided we could escape the tsetse and were not cut off by savage enemies, we might expect to obtain full loads of tusks. Besides three Hottentot drivers and a dozen Makololo, Mr Welbourn was accompanied by a white hunter, Hans Scarff, who had joined him on his way from the coast. His appearance was not in his favour, for a more sinister countenance I had seldom met with. He, however, was said to be a bold hunter and a first-rate horseman, and his assistance was therefore likely to prove useful.

The head man of the Makololoes, Toko, as he was called, was a fine, tall, active fellow with an intelligent countenance, who, if not handsome according to our notion, was good-looking for a black, and a brave faithful fellow. Besides the oxen to drag the waggons, we had eight fine horses, most of them well trained to encounter the elephant and rhinoceros, or any other wild beasts of the forest.

Near our camp a stream of clear water fell into the river, and in the evening Harry asked me to go down and bathe. Hans said he would join us.

"Are there no crocodiles there?" I asked, and I told him of the numbers I had seen in the river.

"No fear of the brutes there," answered Hans; "the water is too shallow —"

"Or hippopotami," I put in.

"Still less likely," said Hans. "The monsters never come up such streams as these."

We started off, and on reaching the stream separated from each other. While looking out for a clear pool free from lilies, or other aquatic plants, presently. Harry, who had gone up the stream, cried out—

"I've found a capital place. We can leap into deep water from the bank."

Just then I heard my uncle shout out—

"Where are you going, boys? The crocodiles come up here to lay their eggs. It is as dangerous a part as any in the country."

At that moment Harry shouted out, "Hulloa! I'm in!"

I was rushing to his assistance, when I heard a fearful cry from Hans, who, his foot slipping, had fallen into the water. As he did so, a huge crocodile darted across the stream.

My uncle and Mr Welbourn were descending the bank, and were much nearer than I was. I was undecided to whose assistance I should run, when, to my horror, I saw the crocodile seize Hans by the arm, before he could regain his feet. I fortunately had my large hunting-knife in my

"I SAW THE CROCODILE SEIZE HANS BY THE ARM."

belt, though I had not; brought my rifle. Little as I liked Hans, I felt that it was my duty to go to his assistance. Unless I did so he would be quickly dragged off into deep water, and become the prey of the crocodile. Seeing that his father and my uncle had already got hold of Harry, drawing my hunting-knife I dashed forward, shouting with all my might to try to frighten the savage brute. Hans had caught hold of the branch of a fallen tree, which he grasped with his left arm, holding on to it for his life. Every moment I expected to see him let go, when his fate would have been sealed. Not for an instant did I think of the danger I was running. I can scarcely even now understand how I acted as I did. With a single bound I sprang over the branches close to the head of the crocodile, and seizing the man with one hand, I plunged the knife into the eye of the monster, who immediately opened his jaws, and as he did so, Hans, with an activity I could scarcely have expected, hauled himself up to the top of the bough, where I sprang after him, while the crocodile, giving a whisk of his tail which nearly knocked us off our perch, retreated into deep water, the next instant to turn lifeless on its back, when, floating down a few yards, its huge body was brought up by a ledge of rocks which projected partly out of the water.

"Well done, Fred, my boy," shouted my uncle and Mr Welbourn in chorus.

Having placed Harry on the bank they hurried forward to assist me in lifting Hans off the bough to which he was clinging, and to place him beside Harry. For some seconds he lay, scarcely knowing what had happened. On examining his arm, though it was fearfully crushed, wonderful as it may seem, no bone was actually broken. After a little time he revived, and, accompanied by Harry, we led him back to the camp. My uncle exerted all his medical skill to doctor him, and the next morning, though his arm was useless, he was able to move about as well as ever. He did not exhibit any special feeling of gratitude to me, but I won the good opinion of the natives, and of Toko in particular. Had anybody told me that I should have been able to perform the act, I should have declared it was impossible, and all I know is that I did it.

As all the ivory in the neighbourhood for which we had goods to give in exchange had been purchased, we pushed forward to the north-east to a country inhabited by tribes which had hitherto had little or no intercourse with Europeans. It is not, however, my object so much to describe the people as the adventures we met with. I cannot exactly say with the naval officer, who, describing the customs of the people he visited, in his journal wrote, "Of manners they have none, and their customs are beastly." Savage those we met were in many respects, but their savagery arose from their ignorance and gross idolatry.

We travelled in a very luxurious manner, compared to our journey with the single ox across the desert. As we advanced we saw numbers of large game, and one evening nearly a hundred buffaloes defiled before us in slow procession, almost within gun-shot, while herds of elands passed us without showing any signs of fear. We at the moment had abundance of meat in the camp, or some of them would have fallen victims to our fire-arms.

The next day, seeing a herd of zebras in the distance, taking my rifle, I started off, hoping to shoot one of them. As the wind was from them to me, and as there were some low bushes, I expected to get up to them within gun-shot, before they perceived me. I was not disappointed; and, firing, I wounded one of them severely in the leg. The rest of the herd took to flight, but the wounded animal went off towards our camp, from which several of our men issued to attack it.

I was walking along leisurely when, hearing the sound of feet in the direction from which I had come, I turned round and saw a solitary buffalo galloping towards me. The nearest place of safety was a tree, but it was upwards of a hundred yards off. I had, of course, reloaded, and now got my rifle ready, hoping to hit the brute in the forehead. Just then the thought occurred to me, "What would be my fate should my gun miss fire?" The buffalo came on at a tremendous speed, but fortunately a small bush in its way made it swerve slightly and expose its shoulder. Now was the moment for action, and as I heard the bullet strike the animal I fell flat on my face. The buffalo bounded on over my body, apparently not perceiving me. I lay perfectly still. It had got to a considerable distance, when it was met by the men who had come out to kill the zebra, and was quickly shot down.

Toko shook his head when he saw me, exclaiming that I must not go out again without him, lest I should be killed by some savage animal.

"But I have my rifle to defend myself," I observed.

"Your rifle may miss fire sometimes, or you may fail to kill the elephant or rhinoceros you attack better have two rifles. I will go with you," he answered, in his peculiar lingo.

Our plan was always to encamp near water, and where we could obtain wood for our fires; for such regions were certain to be frequented by a variety of animals. Sometimes we remained two or three days in the same spot, provided no villages were near; though people were generally grateful to us for destroying the wild beasts, as even the elephants are apt to injure their plantations by breaking in and trampling over them.

Harry and I, who had become fast friends, generally went out together, accompanied by Toko, sometimes on foot, sometimes on horseback. One day we had all three gone out on foot, prepared for any game. That we might be more likely to fall in with some creature or other, we separated a short distance; keeping, however, within hail, and agreeing that, should one of us shout, the other two were to close in towards him. I was in the centre, Toko on the left, and Harry on the right.

We had gone some distance when I heard Toko shout, "Elephant, elephant!" I uttered the same cry to Harry, but he did not apparently hear me, and, at all events, I could not see him. After running for thirty or forty yards, I caught sight of Toko up a tree. He cried out to me to climb another a short distance off, the branches of which would afford an easy ascent. Wishing to follow his advice, I was running along, when my foot caught in a creeper and I fell to the ground with considerable force, letting my rifle drop as I did so, but in vain attempted to regain my legs, so severely had I sprained my ankle. I naturally called to Toko to come to my assistance. He did not move or reply, but continued shouting and shrieking at the top of his voice. What was my horror just then to see a huge elephant, with trunk uplifted, burst out from among the trees on one side, while, at the same moment, a large lion approached with stealthy steps on the other. I gave myself up for lost, expecting to be carried off in the jaws of the lion, or trampled to death by the feet of the elephant. Toko sat immovable, with his rifle levelled at the lion's head, and just as the brute was about to make its fatal spring he fired. As he did so, I saw the elephant, startled by the sound, swerve on one side, its feet passing close to where I lay, but it did not appear even to see me. Away it went, trumpeting loudly and crashing through the underwood.

The next instant Toko leaped down from his perch and hurried towards me, when, turning my head, I caught sight of the lion struggling on its back, and attempting to regain its feet. Toko, lifting me in his arms, carried me a few paces off, and taking up my rifle again approached the lion and shot it dead. Almost at the same instant the sound of another rifle reached our ears.

"Go and help Harry," I said to Toko; "he may want your assistance."

"I place you in safer place dan dis," he answered; and, again taking me up, he propped me against the root of a large tree close by; then reloading my rifle, he put it into my hands. He next reloaded his own.

"I must go and help Harry," he said; and away he bounded.

I had wished him to go and assist my friend, but scarcely had he disappeared than the dreadful idea came into my head that another lion—companion of the one just killed—might be prowling about and discover me. In spite of the pain I suffered, I endeavoured to rise on my knees, so that should one appear I might take a better aim than I could lying down. Still, should my apprehensions be realised, I felt that I should be placed in a very dangerous predicament. One thing, however, was certain, that it could not be worse than the one from which I had just escaped. Few people have been situated as I have been, with a lion about to spring from one side, and an elephant appearing on the other.

Doing my best to keep up my spirits, I listened attentively to try and ascertain what was happening to Harry. Presently there was more loud trumpeting and directly afterwards two shots were fired in rapid succession. This assured me that Harry had escaped and that Toko had reached the scene of action. The Makololo was too clever and experienced an elephant hunter to be taken at disadvantage, and I had great hopes that he had succeeded in killing the animal.

I did not forget my fears about another lion, and cast my eyes anxiously around almost expecting to see one emerge from the thicket, while at the same time I looked out eagerly for the return of my friend.

Once more the trumpeting burst forth, the sounds echoing through the forest. I thus knew that the elephant had not yet fallen. A minute afterwards I heard the crashing of boughs and brushwood some way off. I guessed, as I listened, that the animal was coming towards where I lay. The sounds increased in loudness. Should it discover me it would probable revenge itself by crushing me to death, or tossing me in the air with its trunk. I had my rifle ready to fire. There was a chance that I might kill it or make it turn aside. The ground where I lay sloped gradually downwards to a more open spot. I expected the next instant that the elephant would appear. It did so, but further off than I thought it would, and I thus began to hope that I should escape its notice. It was moving slowly, though trumpeting with pain and rage. The instant I caught sight of it another huge creature rushed out of the thicket on the opposite side of the glade. It was a huge bull rhinoceros with a couple of sharp-pointed horns one behind the other.

The elephant on seeing it stopped still, as if wishing to avoid a contest with so powerful an antagonist, I fully expected to witness a long and terrible fight, and feared that, in the struggle, the animals might move towards where I lay and crush me. That the elephant was wounded I could see by the blood streaming down its neck. This probably made it less inclined to engage in a battle with the rhinoceros. Instead of advancing it stood whisking its trunk about and trumpeting. The rhinoceros, on the contrary, after regarding it for a moment, rushed fearlessly forward and drove its sharp-pointed horns into its body while it in vain attempted to defend itself with its trunk. The two creatures were now locked together in a way which made it seem impossible for them to separate, unless the horns of the rhinoceros were broken off. Never did I witness a more furious fight. The elephant attempted to throw itself down on the head of its antagonist, and thereby only drove the horns deeper into its own body. So interested was I, that I forgot the pain I was suffering, while I could hear no other sounds than those produced by the two huge combatants. While I was watching them, I felt a hand on my shoulder, and saw Harry standing over me.

"I am sorry you have met with this accident!" he exclaimed. "The sooner you get away from this the better. There is a safer spot a little higher up the bank, Toko and I will carry you there."

I willingly consenting, my friends did as they proposed, as from thence I could watch the fight with greater security. They, having placed me in safety, hurried towards the combatants, hoping to kill both of them before they separated.

The elephant, already wounded, appeared likely to succumb without our further interference. There was indeed little chance of its attempting to defend itself against them. Toko, making a sign to Harry to remain where he was, sprang forward until he got close up to the animals, and firing he sent a bullet

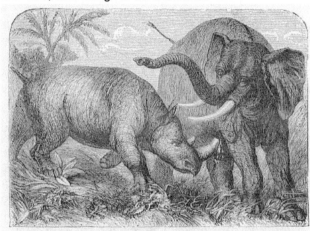

"THE RHINOCEROS DROVE ITS HORNS INTO ITS BODY." [A 116.

right through the elephant's heart. The huge creature fell over, pressing the rhinoceros to the ground. Leaping back Toko again loaded, and Harry advancing they fired together into the body of the survivor, which after giving a few tremendous struggles, sank down dead.

The battle over, Harry proposed carrying me at once to the camp, and then returning to bring away the elephant's tusks, the lion's skin, and as much of the meat of the two first animals as was required for the use of the party. I was very thankful to accept his offer, as I wanted to get my ankle looked to, having an uncomfortable fear that it was broken, in which case my hunting would be put a stop to for many a week to come. He and Toko were not long in manufacturing a litter to carry me, by means of two long poles, on their shoulders. Having placed me on it they set off for the camp. Fortunately we had not very far to go. I hoped that in the mean time we should meet with neither elephants nor lions.

Only under rare circumstances are rhinoceroses to be dreaded, for they are generally mild and well-disposed creatures, and usually take to flight when they come in sight of human beings.

We had gone about half-way, when a lion, bursting out from a thicket close by, stalked across the path some distance ahead. My bearers placed me on the ground and handled their rifles.

"We'll stand by and defend you, don't be alarmed," cried Harry.

"I'm not afraid of your running away," I answered, "but don't fire at the creature unless it approaches to attack us. If you only wound it, its rage may be excited, and I to a certainty shall become its victim."

The lion regarded us for a few seconds when—we raising a loud shout —it, greatly to my satisfaction, bounded on and disappeared in the wood. Indeed a lion when alone will seldom, especially in the day-time, attack human beings who show a bold front, though it will follow like a cat, as do most other savage brutes, if a man runs from it.

My friends again taking me up, we proceeded, though I own that I peered somewhat anxiously into the wood where the lion had retreated, lest it should change its mind and rush out upon us.

My uncle returned soon after we reached the camp, and at once examined my ankle. Greatly to my relief he assured me that it was not broken, and that, if he bound it up in a water bandage, I should probably be well in a day or two. As it was already late, the blacks were unwilling to go through the forest at night for the purpose of bringing in our spoils, for fear of being carried off by lions. All night long we could hear them muttering and roaring. Harry suggested that they were mourning for their late companion. Occasionally the death-cry of some unfortunate deer which they had pulled down reached our ears, while various other sounds, some produced by insects or bullfrogs, or birds, disturbed the silence of the forest. I, however, managed, in spite of the noise and the pain I suffered, to go to sleep, and in the morning, greatly to my satisfaction, I found my ankle much better than I expected.

As meat was wanted, several of the party proposed to set off at an early hour to bring in some from the animals we had killed; my uncle, Mr Welbourn, and Harry going also. As I did not like to be left behind, I begged to be allowed to mount a horse and to ride with them. I should have been wiser to have remained quietly at the camp, but I wanted to revisit the scene of our encounter the previous day. Jan followed behind with several of the blacks, who were to be loaded with our spoils. As we neared the spot, I heard my friends exclaiming in various tones—

"Where is it? What has become of the creature!"—and, pushing forward, I caught sight of the elephant and the dead lion at a distance, but nowhere was the rhinoceros to be seen. It was very evident that it could not have been killed as we had supposed, and that, having only been stunned, it, at length recovering itself, had made off.

Toko cried out that he had discovered its spoor, and I saw him hurrying forward evidently hoping to find the creature. The other blacks meanwhile set to work to cut out the tusks, and select a few slices off such parts of the body as were most to their taste, including the feet, the value of which we knew from experience.

While they were thus occupied, my three white friends were busy in flaying the lion. I kept my eye on Toko, expecting that, should he discover the rhinoceros, he would summon some of the party to his assistance. I saw him look suspiciously into a thicket, then he turned to fly. The next moment a huge beast rushed out, which I had no doubt was the rhinoceros we fancied that we had killed on the previous day. Toko made for a tree behind which he could shelter himself. I called to my friends to draw their attention to the danger in which he was placed, but to my dismay before he could reach the tree the rhinoceros was upon him. There was no time to leap either to the one side or the other, but as the animal's sharp horn was about to transfix him, he made a spring as if to avoid it, but he was not in time, and the animal, throwing up its head, sent him and his rifle floating into the air to the height of several feet. The rhinoceros then charged on towards the men cutting up the elephant, when my uncle and his companions, having seized their rifles, began blazing away at it. Fortunately one of their shots took effect, and before it had reached the blacks, down it sank to the ground. While Harry hastened on to where Toko lay, my uncle and Mr Welbourn, quickly reloading, fired into its head and finished its existence.

I had ridden up to the Makololo, expecting to find every bone in his body broken. As I approached, to my satisfaction I saw him get up; and though he limped somewhat, after shaking himself and picking up his rifle, he declared that he was not much the worse for the fearful toss he had received, and was as ready as ever for work.

He soon rejoined the rest of the men, and assisted in packing the oxen with the tusks and meat. Some of the flesh of the rhinoceros was also cut off, and with the lion-skin packed up. Rhinoceros meat, though tough, is of good flavour. The portions we carried off were from the

upper part of the shoulder   "THE ANIMAL SENT HIM INTO THE AIR."   [A. 125   and

from the ribs, where we found the fat and lean regularly striped to the depth of two inches. Some of the skin was also taken for the purpose of making some fresh ox-whips. We of course carried away the horns, which are about half the value of ivory. Altogether, the adventure which at one time appeared likely to prove so disastrous, afforded us no small amount of booty.

Chapter Seven.

The constant mutterings and roarings which saluted our ears during the night, made us suspect that we should not obtain much game in the neighbourhood, besides which we should run a great risk of being attacked while out shooting. We therefore struck camp, and proceeded on to the northward. The country in many places was rocky, and though there were no mountains of any great height there were savage defiles through which we had to pass, the sides of the cliffs being covered with brushwood and creepers, and in some spots with tall trees. We were not afraid of being attacked by natives, but notwithstanding we always sent out scouts on our flanks and ahead.

We had gone on some distance when Toko, who was leading, came hurrying back.

"I have seen a strange sight, which I would rather not have seen," he exclaimed.

"What is it?" asked my uncle.

"Lions, a whole army of them. They seem determined to stop our way," he answered.

"If there were a hundred of them they should not

"LIONS, A WHOLE ARMY OF THEM." [p. 16. do that," replied my uncle. "We'll have a look at the gentlemen. We shall soon drive them off if I mistake not."

As it would have been imprudent to carry the cattle and horses into the neighbourhood, a halt was called, and the blacks were left in charge of the animals, while we, with Hans Scarff, prepared to ride forward.

"Stay!" said Harry. "I think we have got something to send them to the rightabout, if our shouts fail to drive them away." And going to the waggon he produced half-a-dozen rockets.

"One of those will do," observed his father, "for we may want the rest for another emergency. However, you can carry a couple in case one should fail."

Led by Toko, we proceeded along the defile, when, on reaching some high ground, we saw, collected together below us among the rocks, an immense number of lions. There must have been several families, fathers and mothers with their young ones. What could have brought them together to that spot, it was difficult to conjecture. Toko declared that they knew we were about to pass that way, and had assembled for the purpose of attacking us. Of course such an idea was ridiculous;

66

however, there they were, and had we passed close to them, they might have committed serious havoc among our cattle, although we should no doubt have shot down many of them. They must have seen us, from the way they lashed their tails and muttered; while, from the loud roars which three or four of the elders gave forth, it was pretty clear that they meant mischief.

We, however, rode forward determined to drive them away. Harry and I, in the meantime, got the rockets ready to fire in case our shouts should fail to produce the desired effect. As we got nearer there was a general movement among them. As we shouted they roared in return, apparently not being alarmed by the sound of our voices.

"We must not remain unarmed, so let only three fire at a time, while the others reload," said my uncle. "Now fire!"

As the smoke cleared away, it seemed doubtful whether any of the shots had taken effect, as the lions did not move from the spot they occupied.

"I suspect they are waiting for the appearance of a herd of'gemsboks,' and that they will not give up the chance of catching their prey," observed my uncle.

"We must disappoint them then," said Mr Welbourn. "Harry, get one of your rockets ready, and pitch it into the middle of them directly after we fire our next volley."

We had got the tube fixed and placed at the proper elevation. We had to wait until those next to fire had discharged their rifles, when two of the lions were evidently badly wounded, but even this did not make them take to flight. Harry then applied the match to the rocket which pitched in the midst of the congregated lions. The effect was electrical. Seized with a panic, away they all scampered over the rocks at a greater rate than I had ever before seen lions run. None stopped for the others. One with his spine injured lay on the ground. Two others dropped before they had got far, while the remainder were soon out of sight.

"The brutes will not come back to this locality," exclaimed my uncle. "We must now put the other ones out of their pain."

A rifle ball sent through the head of each quickly did this. Rapidly skinning them, we left the carcases to be devoured by the birds of prey, which almost before we got out of sight appeared in the air; for although hyaenas and jackals are said to keep aloof even from a dead lion, the vulture tribes possess no such awe for the monarch of the wilds.

Returning to where we had left our cattle, we at once moved forward, anxious to get out from among the rocky defiles as soon as possible. Scarcely had we emerged from them, than we saw in the distance an enormous herd of deer, which Mr Welbourn at once pronounced to be "pallah." As they approached we drew on one side before we were discovered. First came a stag, a magnificent animal of a bay colour, fading into a whitey-brown, with elegantly, somewhat harp-shaped horns, marked with rings, and a black semi-circular mark on the croup by which it could be at once distinguished. Its feet were of a jetty hue. Though it might have seen us, it continued walking on in a sedate manner, the rest following their leader with a confidence which showed that they must put implicit trust in him.

My uncle and Hans, at once dismounting, crept towards the herd; and, waiting until the greater number had passed, fired together, when three of the animals fell dead. The remainder, instead of turning to fly, dashed forward to fill up the gaps in their line, the whole moving on at a much greater speed than before. Two others, however, were killed before the herd made their escape through the pass towards which they were directing their course.

Had we not driven away the lions, probably many more would have been killed by them. We at once carried off the five which were destined for provisioning our party, and loaded our waggons with their skins and horns.

We were now approaching a part of the country where we hoped to find a greater number of elephants than we had yet met with, our chief object being to obtain their tusks; although nothing came amiss, rhinoceros horns, skins, or ostrich feathers; the latter especially, from their small bulk, were really of more value than elephant tusks.

We were now crossing a wide plain with rocks. Here and there were ant-hills, by the side of each of which grew a dark-leaved tree called the "Mollopie." Near our camp was a rain-pool, at which our animals were watered. Jan here captured a large frog in which, when he cut it open, for the purpose of preparing it for cooking, he found a whole mouse, two or three ants, and several other insects.

In the morning our people informed us that they had heard the roaring of a lion during the night at a neighbouring pool; and as there was a great likelihood of his paying a visit to the camp, to make a feast off our oxen, we determined to dispatch him before going out to hunt.

As we approached the pool, the noise was again heard.

"He must be in a thicket close by," exclaimed Harry.

But every thicket round was well beaten, and no lion appeared. At last I heard Harry laughing heartily, and saw him pointing to the opposite side of the pool, where I caught sight of a big frog poking his head above the reeds. There could be no doubt of it. Though he could not swell himself to the size of a lion, Mr Bullfrog had managed to imitate very closely his voice, so we returned to camp feeling somewhat ashamed of ourselves, Harry every now and then giving way to a burst of laughter.

In the open country, where little shelter is to be found, lions are not often to be met with, and as they can be seen long before they approach, no danger is to be apprehended from them. One of the men who had remained behind followed, bringing one of the bullfrogs which he had captured in the pool. The body, which we measured, was nine inches in length, by five and a half wide; and the hind legs, from toe to toe, eighteen inches. On being cut open a young bird which it had lately swallowed was found in its inside.

I, having completely recovered the use of my foot, arranged with Harry that we should make another expedition together in search of game. We agreed that Jan should accompany us, and just as we were starting Hans offered to go. We would rather have dispensed with his company, as he was not a favourite with either of us. Mr Welbourn, my uncle, Toko, and two or three Makololoes were to set off in another direction. They charged us not to go beyond a *vlei* or pool, which we had heard of from the Makololoes, about twelve miles to the northward.

"FIRST CAME A STAG, A MAGNIFICENT ANIMAL." [p. 136.

This, however, gave us a very wide scope, and we fully expected to come back with plenty of game of some sort.

We went on for some distance without meeting with any live creatures, though we crossed the spoor of numerous elands, buffaloes, giraffes, and occasionally of elephants. Neither Hans nor Jan knew more of the country than we did, but Harry said that he had brought a compass, so that we should have no difficulty in finding our way, even should clouds gather in the sky or night overtake us. When, however, he came to search for the instrument in his pocket, it was not to be found.

"Never mind," he observed, "as the sky is bright, the sun will guide us by day, and the stars by night, even if we are kept out, and there is no reason why we should be if we turn back again in good time."

On we went, therefore, intending on arriving at the *vlei*, to wait until some animals should come to drink, which they were sure to do, unless there were other water-holes in the neighbourhood.

We had brought very little food, expecting to be able to supply ourselves with meat and fruits. From the appearance of the country we had no doubt that we should meet with melons, even though we might not come across water before we arrived at the *vlei*.

We had, according to our calculation, gone about two-thirds of the distance without having shot a single animal, when the weather began to change. Clouds gathered in the sky, and a thick mist swept across the face of the country, such as occasionally, though not often, occurs in that latitude. We agreed, however, that by turning directly back we

70

should have to traverse the same region we had just passed over, without finding game, and we should thus be disappointed in obtaining food. This was not to be thought of. I would be far better to go on to where we should have every chance of finding it. Hans concurred with us, and, as Jan was always ready to go forward, on we went.

In consequence of being shaded from the rays of the sun, we were better able to travel than usual during the hot hours of the day. We had reached the part of the country where we had expected to find the *vlei*; but, even though Jan mounted to the topmost boughs of the tallest tree we could find, when he came down he declared that he could not discover water.

We therefore again pushed on, until we reached a rocky hill, to the summit of which we climbed. Not a pool could we see either to the north, east, south, or west.

We were now getting both hungry and thirsty, for we had exhausted the water we had brought in our bottles. We were convinced, however, that we must be near the *vlei*, and that some rise in the ground probably hid it from view. While looking about we caught sight of some animals of the deer tribe, and Harry and I arranged to go down to try and kill one of them, while Hans and Jan were to continue the search for water, and, should they find it, they were to meet us at the foot of the hill, from which they started.

Keeping ourselves among the rocks and shrubs and tall grass, we made our way in the direction we had seen the deer. As we got nearer Harry pronounced them to be *ourebis*. We were afraid that we should have no chance of getting within shot, for we saw them gliding rapidly along, often bounding several feet into the air, then galloping on again, and once more bounding on.

"I'll try a dodge I once saw practised," whispered Harry. "Do you lie down with your rifle ready to fire behind yonder bush, and I'll go forward and show myself. They have a good deal of curiosity in their nature, and I'll try to excite it."

He then placed his rifle and coat and hat on the ground, and creeping a little forward, to one side of where I lay, he suddenly rose with his feet in the air, supporting himself on his hands. How he could manage to maintain that position so long surprised me. I should have had the blood rush into my head and dropped down in a minute had I made the attempt.

All the time I was watching the ourebis; which, no longer leaping about, remained quiet for some seconds, and then with slow and stately steps advanced towards the curious object. I had time to examine them minutely. Their colour was a pale tawny above, and white below. The horns straight and pointed, and, as far as I could judge, five inches in length. The animal itself is of no great height, standing not more than two feet from the ground, though when it lifts up its head it looks much taller. The female of the pair which approached was hornless. On they came, closer and closer. I was afraid that Harry would drop down and frighten them away before they had got near enough to enable me to take a sure aim.

I was in as good a position as I could desire, for, though the bush effectually concealed me, I could see them clearly. I dared not, however, move my rifle in the least degree, for fear it should touch the leaves and make the animals suspicious. "Do not fire until they begin to move away, I want to get them up close to me," said Harry, in a whisper.

The animals still, in spite of the danger, came on, until they were not twenty yards off. At length, it seemed to me, by the way they moved their ears, that they were on the point of starting.

I fired, the buck dropped on his fore-legs, and at the same instant Harry threw himself on his feet, lifted his rifle and fired at the doe before she had got ten paces off. Down she also came utterly helpless, and was quickly put out of her suffering by Harry. The buck instinctively attempted to defend himself with his horns, but seizing one of them, I deprived him of existence.

We had good reason to be satisfied with the result of Harry's experiment. He told me that not only the ourebis but several other deer, if attracted in the same way by their suspicions or curiosity being aroused, can be thus shot.

We lost no time in cutting open our deer, so as to lighten the loads, and the better to preserve the meat. Each was as much as a man could carry on his shoulders. We were unwilling, however, to leave any part behind. Believing that we could carry

"ON THEY CAME, CLOSER AND CLOSER." [p. 137.] them better whole than cut up, we staggered along with our burdens, fortunately not having far to go. On arriving at the spot agreed on, we found that our companions had not returned. We therefore set to work to collect fuel for a fire, and to cut up one of the animals. So parched had we become, that we could scarcely refrain from drinking their blood. I had always found, however, that blood rather increased than diminished thirst. We were both by this time well versed in wood-craft, and quickly divided the animal in the most scientific fashion. While we were employed in this manner, we frequently looked round to ascertain if the two men were approaching, but they were not to be seen.

Having finished our task, while I was making up the fire, Harry climbed to the top of the rock, that he might obtain a wider look-out.

"I can see them nowhere," he said, when he came down, "but I caught sight of an animal which, if I mistake not, is a big lion following our spoor, or probably it is attracted by the scent of the deer. As he is coming this way, we must be prepared for him: though he might not condescend to eat a dead deer, he may take it into his head to carry off one of us living subjects. He is not likely to give us any undue notice of his approach."

Harry agreed therefore to keep watch while I continued the operations on which I was engaged. I soon got some forked sticks, which I ran into the ground to hold the spits, and on these I placed the venison to roast, but hungry as I was I felt that without water I could scarcely get down the food I was cooking. Evening was approaching.

"I say, Fred, if those fellows don't come soon, we must set off by ourselves, and look out for water. Perhaps some may be found among the rocks, or if not, we must cut some wooden spades and dig for it. Those deer wouldn't be inhabiting these parts if water wasn't in the neighbourhood."

"It will be too late to commence any search tonight," I observed. "It is already nearly dark, and the chances are that the lion you saw just now will pounce down upon us, if we go far from the fire. I would rather endure thirst than run that risk."

"Still we must have water," exclaimed Harry; "but you stay here and look after the venison, and I'll just wander to a short distance. I do not suppose the brute will find me; and perhaps, you know, it was not a lion after all I saw: it might have been a buffalo or a brindled gnu."

"You said positively it was a lion," I remarked; "for your own sake, as well as mine, I beg that you will not wander from the camp."

Still Harry, pointing to his mouth, insisted on going. Just as he was about to set off, a loud roar, not twenty paces off, reached our ears.

"What do you say now?" I asked. "You don't mean to assert that that was the cry either of an ostrich or a bullfrog."

"I wish that it were the latter," he answered; "for then there would be a chance of finding water. However, I'll stay in camp and try to endure my thirst until those fellows come back—and they're pretty sure to find water."

I did not like to say that I was not quite certain on that subject. I had hopes, however, that even should they have failed to find it, we should not perish, as I trusted before long we might have a shower of rain, although none had as yet fallen from the cloudy sky. Some venison which I had put close to the fire was by this time cooked, but it was with the greatest difficulty that we could get down even a few mouthfuls.

"I cannot eat another morsel," cried Harry, putting down his knife. "If those fellows don't arrive soon, dark as it is, I must set off by myself to try and find water; depend upon it, there is some not far off, or that lion would not come here," and he threw himself, utterly overcome, on the ground.

I tried to cheer him up, and made another attempt to eat some venison, but had to give it up after nibbling at a piece; yet I felt that I could have swallowed a hearty meal, if I could have obtained a draught of water, however tepid and full of insects it might have been.

We were sitting a short distance from the fire with our rifles in our hands, prepared for the reception of the lion, should he venture to invade our camp, when Harry exclaimed, "Hark! I hear footsteps: they must be those of Hans and your black fellow."

We listened; and I hoped that Harry was right.

"Let us shout!" I exclaimed.

We both together raised our voices. Our hail was answered from a distance. The night air had brought the sound of footsteps much further than I should have supposed possible. It was some time before, by the light of the fire, we saw the rough, uncouth figure of Hans, followed by Jan.

"Have you brought water?" was the first question Harry asked.

"Yah! we have brought water, and have seen plenty of elephants—fine country for shooting, and we will go there to-morrow."

"Never mind the elephants and shooting now; hand me the water," cried Harry, eagerly.

Hans gave Harry his skin bottle, and Jan hurried up with his to me. I swallowed the liquid eagerly, hot and nauseous as it was, full, I suspect, of living creatures; but it tasted like nectar, and I half emptied the bottle at a draught.

"Now I am ready for the venison!" cried Harry.

"So am I, indeed," said Hans; "for we haven't had anything to eat once we left you, and are well-nigh dying of starvation."

"As we were of thirst," I remarked, handing Hans and Jan a large piece of venison each. They devoured it eagerly, and Harry and I then turned to and were able to eat a good meal.

"I should like to get some sleep," said Hans; "we will tell you to-morrow of our adventures."

"We are in no hurry to hear them," said Harry; "but I tell you, one of us must keep a watch, or we may have an unpleasant visit from a lion,

75

who is prowling about in the neighbourhood."

"The cowardly brute won't come near us," said Hans, drowsily. "The chances are it was a rock you saw in the dusk, or it might have been a jackal."

"But we heard it roar," said Harry.

"Oh, then it was a bullfrog," cried Hans, rolling himself up in his cloak and lying down.

"Bullfrog or lion, there it is again!" exclaimed Harry, jumping up and seizing his rifle.

There was no doubt about the matter; though the voice of an ostrich at a distance may sound like that of a lion, the roar of the king of the forest is unmistakable when close at hand. Even Hans was convinced, and was quickly on his feet. It was very certain that we should get no rest that night, unless we could dispose of the intruder. The lion-skin was also of value, and we could not allow him to escape with impunity. We all advanced together, resolved forthwith to shoot the brute; that we should see him directly we had no doubt. A short distance off, between our camp-fire and the spot whence the roar proceeded, was a pile of low rocks, a spur from a neighbouring hill. We had just reached it, when we caught sight of the lion who had emerged from behind a thicket a little way ahead. He seemed at once to look upon us as his foes. Had it been in the day-time, he would probably have slunk away; but night was his season for activity; and, lashing his tail and again roaring loudly, he advanced across the open space below the rocks. Now was the critical moment: should we fail to kill him, he might make a desperate spring and knock over one of us. It was settled, therefore, that Harry and Jan should fire first, and then Hans and I, should they fail to kill the brute: we to try what we could do, they, of course, in the meantime, reloading.

The grand principle in attacking wild beasts is never to allow the whole of the party to remain unarmed for a moment. The lion did not appear quite to like the look of things. He advanced cautiously, showing his whole vast proportions, his huge shaggy mane, and the afterpart of his body looking thin and small, but even that was of the size of a full-grown donkey. Twice he stopped, and each time uttered a tremendous roar.

"He smells us, if he cannot see us," said Harry.

Still the creature appeared doubtful whether he would spring towards the suspected point.

"Now, Harry, let's see what you can do," I whispered.

"I shall be glad if I can knock him over the first shot," he answered.

Harry and Jan's rifles went off at the same moment, and we could hear their bullets strike, but neither brought the lion to the ground. His rage overcame his fears; and lashing his tail and again roaring, he was about to spring on us, when Hans and I, taking steady aim at him as he rose from the ground, sent our leaden messengers of death through his body. He must have leapt up half-a-dozen feet, falling right over on his head, where he lay struggling for a few seconds; but before we could leap over the rocks and get near him, he was dead. We signified our satisfaction at the victory by a loud shout.

"We shall now sleep soundly," said Hans, giving the animal a kick with his foot.

We repaired to our camp and made up the fire. Though Hans declared that   there   was   no   necessity   for

"HARRY AND JAN'S RIFLES WENT OFF AT THE SAME MOMENT." [A. 146.] remaining awake, Harry and I agreed to keep watch and watch until the morning, not feeling at all certain whether another lion, or perhaps a leopard, might pay us a visit; or a herd of elephants, buffaloes, or rhinoceroses, might come our way and trample us to death, while enjoying our balmy slumbers.

Chapter Eight.

When people know that their lives may depend upon maintaining a blazing fire, they must be foolish indeed if they allow themselves to slumber at their posts; but I confess that I had great difficulty, during my watch, in keeping my eyes open, after the exertions of the day and the hunger and thirst I had endured. I felt that my only chance was to get up and walk about with my rifle in my hand. I did not, however, go far from the fire, as the smoke drove the mosquitoes and other insects away from its immediate vicinity; and I knew also, that at any distance from the flames I was as likely to be seized by a savage animal as I should be did no fire exist.

I could hear every now and then the mutterings and occasional roars of lions, with the cries of hyaenas and jackals, and the calls of various night-birds. Altogether the concert had a somewhat depressing effect, accustomed though I was by this time to the noises proceeding from an African forest.

At last the time I had agreed to watch came to an end, and I roused up Harry, charging him to keep a bright look-out.

"Do not let yourself drop off for a moment, old fellow," I said; "as long as any prowling animal sees you moving about around the fire he'll not venture to make an attack; but should you slumber for a moment, it is impossible to say what he may do."

"I do feel awfully drowsy, I own," answered Harry, rubbing his eyes and yawning; "still I'll do my best. It is a shame that fellow Hans won't stand watch as he ought to do. I only hope that another lion will come roaring close up to the camp, for the sake of making him get on his legs. He knows that neither you nor I would sleep on our posts, so he rests in perfect security, throwing all the trouble on us."

Harry and I talked on for a little time, I hoping that he would thus be thoroughly aroused; then I lay down on the spot he had occupied, pretty close to the fire, with my rifle by my side ready for instant use.

It appeared to me that I had not been asleep five minutes when I heard Harry exclaim—

"Fred, rouse Jan. Up with you, and get ready for battle."

I seized my rifle and sprang to my feet, as wide awake as ever I was in my life, and there I saw, not six paces off, a creature with glaring eyes; not a lion, however, but looking unusually large as it emerged from the darkness into the light of the fire.

It crouched as if for a spring; at the same moment I heard Hans shriek out. For an instant I glanced round, and caught an indistinct sight of another big cat-like creature stealing towards the rear of the camp.

"You and Jan must look out after that brute, and we'll attend to this one," I shouted.

As I spoke, the leopard, for such it was, notwithstanding our cries,—Harry, I should have said, had begun to bawl away as loudly as I was doing,—made a furious spring towards him; but though he was shouting lustily, he remained as cool as a cucumber, holding his rifle ready.

We fired, and both our balls took effect, when the leopard literally turned, with its feet uppermost, and fell right down into the centre of the fire, where it lay struggling convulsively, utterly unable to rise. Directly afterwards I heard the report of a pistol, and, while hastily reloading, I saw that Hans had shot the other leopard through the head.

As we did not wish to lose the skin of the one we had shot, Harry again firing gave it its quietus; we then seizing it by its hind legs dragged it out of the fire, and Jan's knife soon finished the other.

We thus gained two magnificent leopards' skins: the fire had but slightly injured the one we had killed.

"There is some use in keeping watch at night, Hans," observed Harry; "what would have become of us if I had not been awake? Those brutes would have been in our midst before we were able to lift a hand in our defence. As it was, I caught sight of only one of them stealing towards us, and had barely time to rouse up the rest of you, so that if Fred hadn't been very quick, the brute would have been down upon us."

"All right," answered Hans, "such a thing is not likely to happen a second time in a night, so I suppose we may now go to sleep in quiet."

"I don't suppose anything of the sort," replied Harry; "there are no end of lions and leopards prowling about, and you would have heard them if you hadn't snored so loudly. It will be your turn to keep watch, and I intend to rouse you up in half an hour."

"Yah, yah," answered Hans, placing his head on the ground, and going off to sleep again.

As I thought would probably be the case, the scent of the dead leopards attracted packs of hyaenas and jackals, who serenaded us with their horrible yells and howls for the remainder of the night, though the blazing fire we kept up prevented them from approaching.

Notwithstanding Harry's threat, he did not wake up Hans, who would probably again have composed himself for sleep, and we might have been left to the tender mercies of the hyaenas.

In the morning we took the skins off the two leopards; and cleaned and packed them up so as to be easily transported. As Hans claimed the skin of the leopard he had shot, he had to carry it, while Jan carried ours. We then started off for the *vlei*. It would be too late in the morning, we calculated, by the time we could reach it, to shoot any animals; and we should have to wait till the evening, when they would be likely to come down to drink at the pool. We should not, therefore, have hastened our footsteps, had we not been anxious to obtain a fresh supply of water; for the small stock Hans and Jan had brought was exhausted, and we were now almost as thirsty as we had been on the previous day.

" WE FIRED, AND BOTH OUR BALLS TOOK EFFECT." [p. 131.

Hans walked on ahead without speaking; but as he was never very talkative, we were not surprised at this. At last he turned round, and told Jan that he must carry his leopard-skin.

We thought this too much of a good thing. Jan appealed to us.

"Certainly not," answered Harry. "You claimed all the skin as your property. You are bound to carry it, or leave it behind if you like, but Jan shall not be compelled to carry it."

Hans turned round and walked on sullenly, but presently I saw him drop his burden, and then present his rifle at Harry. Fearing that Hans was about to murder my friend, I dashed forward and struck up the weapon, which the next instant went off, the bullet almost grazing Harry's hat.

"We must overpower the man," I said, making a sign to Jan, and we all three threw ourselves upon him, and prevented him drawing his knife, when he would, I suspect, have run amuck among us, as the Malays frequently do when exasperated.

How to treat the madman—for such he appeared to be—it was difficult to say. He was immensely strong, and we had to exert ourselves to keep him down. Jan proposed to kill him, and was drawing his knife for the purpose when we interfered.

"We shall have to do it, I fear, if we cannot bind his hands behind him," said Harry.

"No, no; we must deprive him of his rifle and ammunition, and he will thus be compelled to follow us."

"If he wanders away into the desert, his fate will be certain," observed Harry.

"He has brought it upon himself," I remarked; "here, Jan, take my rifle-strap; slip it round his arms and draw it tight,—be quick about it. Now, Harry, get another strap round his legs."

All this time Hans was struggling violently, without uttering a word. Having succeeded in doing as I proposed, we had him completely in our power. He grinned fearfully and foamed at the mouth; indeed, he almost seized poor Jan's bare arm in his teeth, and had not Harry given him a severe blow he would have succeeded.

"Now let's try to get him on his feet, and we will then slacken the strap sufficiently to enable him to walk, though not to allow him to run away," I said.

Hans was very unwilling at first to move, but at length we got him to walk along, though he appeared like a man in a dream,—not knowing what he was doing. Jan assured us that he could find the way to the water-hole, and we therefore proceeded in the direction he pointed out. It was a question, however, whether we should remain to shoot there, or, having supplied our bottles, return with our unfortunate companion to the camp. As he seemed strong enough to carry the leopard-skin, we replaced it on his shoulders. Every now and then he would attempt to run; but the strap round his legs quickly brought him up. Our progress was of course very slow, until at length the *vlei* was reached. We passed on our way several trees of considerable size overturned by elephants; many of them being ten inches in diameter, it must have required great strength to uproot them. Others were broken short off, a little distance from the ground, by the elephants. This showed us that the country was frequented by the animals, and that if we had patience we might be able to shoot a number. While lying in ambush, however, it would be necessary to remain perfectly silent, as they would be alarmed by the slightest noise.

At length the water-hole came in sight, and eagerly hurrying forward we quenched our thirst and refilled our bottles. Hans did not refuse to drink, and appeared somewhat better afterwards; but there was a roll in his eye which made us unwilling to set him at liberty. Not to alarm the elephants, we retired to a distance and lighted a fire, where we cooked the venison we had brought with us, which, although somewhat high, was still eatable; we then lay down to rest under the shade of a wide-spreading tree, making Hans sit by us.

Harry and I, wishing to obtain some sleep, told Jan to watch our prisoner; and as he had had more rest than we had the previous night, we hoped he would keep awake.

At length I opened my eyes, and, on looking round, what was my dismay to see Jan fast asleep, and to find that Hans was not there. I aroused Harry. We had placed our prisoner's rifle and knife close to us, and they were safe. He could not be far off; so calling Jan—who looked very much surprised at finding what had happened—we started off, hoping to discover the poor wretch. The feeling of anger with which we had before regarded him was now changed into compassion. Should he have had any evil intentions, could he have got his arms free, he might have brained us as we slept. However, it seemed doubtful whether he had been able to get more than his legs at liberty. The strap which secured his elbows was nowhere to be seen. We traced his spoor, but this disappeared along an elephant track—for even Jan failed to discover the marks of his footsteps. The night was approaching, and we lost all hope of discovering him. We therefore took up our position in the thicket we had selected, close to the path the elephants pursued when going down to the pool. We here fully expected to shoot two or three animals. We then proposed returning next morning to the camp, in order to bring two or three of the men with us to make further search for Hans.

We had not long taken up our position, when we caught sight of the huge forms of several elephants coming through the forest, along the path which we had discovered. We saw them sweeping their trunks backwards and forwards over the ground, evidently suspecting something wrong.

Thirst impelled them forward, however. They approached close to where we lay hidden, and I was just about to fire at the leader, who had magnificent tusks—Harry having agreed to take the next in order —when a loud shout rent the air, and a figure started up directly in front of the animal. It was Hans. His arms were still bound, but he kept leaping about, utterly fearless of the elephants before him. I hesitated for a moment, when the thought struck me,—should I kill the elephant, I might save the life of the unhappy being who seemed to be courting his fate. I pulled the trigger. I could hear the ball strike, but

"THEY NOW OFFERED UNUSUALLY GOOD MARKS TO OUR RIFLES." [p. 163.

what was my horror to see the animal rush forward, and the next moment trample Hans Scarff beneath his feet. A single shriek escaped the miserable man, and then all was silent. Excited as I was, I did not notice that Harry fired at the second elephant at the same moment. His bullet must have entered the animal's brain, for it sank a helpless mass on the ground. The rest of the herd, alarmed by the fate of their leaders, turned round, and with loud trumpeting rushed away into the forest.

The first elephant, in the meantime, lifted up the body of his victim, whom he dashed violently to the ground; and then, staggering a few paces, came down with a crash and lay motionless.

We hurried out of our ambush to render assistance to Hans; but he was dead, every bone in his body being broken; even his features could not be recognised. We could not blame ourselves for the occurrence, though grieved at his sad fate.

We now purposed returning to our last camp, where we had left our fire burning. Jan begged leave to cut off some pieces of the elephant's flesh to cook for supper. This he did forthwith, in a more rapid way than we could have accomplished the task.

Covering up the body of Hans with some thick bushes, we left it where it lay, in order to prevent the hyaenas and jackals from getting at it, and returned to our fire.

We had not long been seated round it, talking over the events of the day, when Jan, starting up, declared that he saw the light of a fire in the distance.

Harry and I looked in the same direction. There was no doubt about the matter.

"Who can they be?" exclaimed Harry.

"Perhaps they are natives," I answered. "If so, we must be careful how we approach them."

"I think it is more likely that they are our friends coming to search for us," said Harry. "They will be surprised at our not appearing yesterday, and may have pushed forward a party who, if on horseback, would soon be up with us."

I at length agreed that such was probably the case, and we accordingly settled at once to go towards the fire. We should probably, even at a distance, be able to discover whether or not it was made by our friends. Jan was of our opinion.

Having hastily finished our meal, we made our way in the direction we proposed. On getting near the fire, Jan offered to go forward and to bring word while we lay hid, so that we might retreat if necessary before we were discovered.

When I was in the forests of Africa, I always remembered that while I was stalking an animal, a lion or leopard might be stalking me; and we therefore, while we waited for the return of Jan, kept our eyes about us, and our ears open to detect the slightest sound.

We had longer to wait than we expected. At length we heard a rustling of leaves near us, and Jan's voice exclaiming—

"Dey de Capt'n's party, and Toko, and two, three, Makololoes; dey all got horses!"

This was good news. As we went along he told me that he had not informed them that we were near, as he wished to give us the pleasure of announcing ourselves.

In a few minutes we were in the midst of our friends, and our appearance afforded my uncle great relief. They had come across our camp, and found the bodies of the lions, and had some misapprehensions that after all we might have been carried off by others.

He was, of course, much shocked at the fate of Hans, though, he observed, that it was better he should have died thus, than have committed murder or some other mischief, as from his uncertain temper it was very likely he would have done.

The Makololoes, on hearing that we had killed two elephants, were eager to go at once and obtain some of the flesh; but my uncle persuaded them to remain until the next morning, promising that they should then have an abundance of meat.

Although expeditions on foot have their advantages, Harry and I came to the conclusion, when we again found ourselves mounted, that we should prefer in future going out on horseback. My uncle told us that he expected the waggons would camp where we then were, so that we might load them with the tusks and skins we might obtain.

Directly breakfast was over we rode to the scene of our encounter with the two elephants, neither of which had been disturbed. The tusks were soon removed, and the Makololoes cut away enough flesh for a whole army. A grave was then dug, and the body of poor Hans buried. This done, we followed the spoor of the elephants, intending to kill them while feeding in the day-time, and afterwards attack them as they came down to drink.

We had not ridden far when Toko, who was ahead, came back with the intelligence that he had discovered four or five in an open glade, plucking off the branches and leaves of their favourite trees; and that by keeping along through the wood we might come upon them without much risk of being discovered. Almost a minute afterwards we came in sight of the animals, when we at once dismounted to watch them and arrange our plan of proceeding. While some Makololoes held our horses, my uncle, Harry, and I crept along not far from the edge of the forest, so as to get in front of the elephants we saw feeding, while Mr Welbourn, Toko, and one of his followers made a wider circuit, with the intention of taking them on the other side should they move in that direction. We hurried on, eager to get in front of the animals before they should move away. They now offered unusually good marks to our rifles. My fear was that their sharp eyes might detect us before we could get near enough to fire. My uncle advised each of us to select a tree up which we could climb, or whose trunk was of sufficient thickness to afford us protection should the elephants, discovering us, make a charge.

As the forest was tolerably thick, they could not move as rapidly as in the open ground. We hoped, therefore, to have time to escape should our bullets fail to kill them at the first shot. There were three magnificent fellows feeding close together, and several others beyond them. The latter had fallen to the share of Mr Welbourn and his party, and we agreed to devote our attention to the three nearest. We proceeded with the greatest care, in Indian file. The slightest sound, even at a distance, caused by a stumble or the breaking of a twig, would attract the attention of our expected prey.

We at length could see their trunks lifted above their heads to reach the higher branches, the rest of their bodies being invisible, and of course they could not see us.

Having taken up our positions, one in front of each elephant, we crept forward, bending down as low as we could so as to escape detection as long as possible. At the same time we looked out for trees to serve as places of refuge. Activity and presence of mind are necessary when a person is hunting wild beasts, but especially when elephant shooting.

I lost sight of my uncle, who was on my left, but I could just see Harry, who was on the opposite side, his head appearing above the grass and shrubs. I had made up my mind not to fire until I heard the report of my uncle's rifle. At last I could see the huge ears of an elephant, just in front of me, flapping up and down.

I knew that the moment would soon arrive when I must fire or be discovered by the elephant. I crept on a few paces further, then rose on my knees. At the moment that I heard the crack of my uncle's rifle, I lifted my own weapon and fired, aiming full at the creature's broad chest as high up as I could, so as to clear the head. Before the smoke —which was kept from rising by the branches—had cleared away, a loud trumpeting was heard. The moment it began Harry

" WHAT WAS OUR SURPRISE TO SEE AN ENORMOUS LION."
[p. 166.

fired, but I could not see the result. I sprang to my feet, so as to escape behind a tree I had marked, fully expecting to have the elephant I had shot charge furiously at me; but it did not, and though I retreated some paces I could still see its head. It seemed to be looking about to discover the enemy who had wounded it. No long time passed before it caught sight of me, and then on it came. I could also hear a loud crashing among the boughs to the right, produced, I had no doubt, by the elephant at which Harry had aimed. On reaching the tree I instantly began to reload, hoping to have time to give the elephant another shot as he passed me; for, though he had seen me for a moment, I knew that he would go straight on without looking behind the tree. But, even before he had got up to the spot, down he fell on his knees, crushing several young trees. At the same

87

moment I heard Harry cry out, and leaving my own prize I dashed forward to his assistance. I was just in time to see the elephant, with his trunk uplifted, close to Harry, who had not had time to reload or take shelter behind a tree. I fired, aiming behind the ear of the elephant, when down it came, as mine had done, prostrate on the ground. If my uncle had been equally successful, we should have made a grand haul. Without stopping to finish off our elephants, we hurried in the direction we supposed him to be, reloading as we went. We uttered a loud shout to attract his attention. It was replied to by a tremendous roar; and, instead of an elephant, what was our surprise to see an enormous lion lashing its tail and looking up at the branches of a tree, among which we discovered my uncle; and he must have had a narrow escape, for he was only just beyond reach of the brute, who might, it seemed to us, by making a desperate spring, have struck him down. We had now to look out for ourselves, for should the lion discover us, unless we could kill him at once, he might tear us to pieces. Fortunately another tree of considerable girth, and in the position we desired, was close at hand. We retreated behind it. As the lion turned his head and we thought might be looking for us, we both fired. To our great delight we rolled him over where he stood.

"Bravo! Well done!" cried my uncle, descending the tree. "We'll now go after my elephant."

Leading the way, without exchanging further words, he dashed out of the forest.

Chapter Nine.

On getting out from among the trees we caught sight of an elephant going along at full swing across the plain. There seemed but little chance of our overtaking him, but my uncle urged us to persevere, for by the large blotches and splashes of blood which we met with, it was evident that he was wounded. It was pretty hot work, as we were loaded with our ammunition and our rifles, but we were encouraged to proceed by finding that the elephant was slackening his pace.

"We shall catch him before long!" exclaimed my uncle. "On, on. If that lion hadn't interfered, I should have shot him at once; but the brute's lair must have been close to where I stood, and I ran a fearful chance of being seized by him."

We did not see what had become of the other elephants, and we concluded that either Mr Welbourn had disposed of them, or that they had run into the forest to conceal themselves. However, we soon saw that the attempt to overtake the elephant on foot was useless. We therefore made a short cut back to where we had left our horses. Each of us mounting one, guided by the spoor, we immediately made chase. It was far more satisfactory to be on horseback than on foot. Following the spoor, we quickly again came in sight of the elephant, which was moving slowly on. Seeing us, he lifted up his trunk and, trumpeting loudly, seemed about to charge.

My uncle, notwithstanding, rode forward and fired. The ball struck, when immediately, turning the horse's head, he galloped off, taking the way towards the camp. He had not gone far, however, before the elephant stopped, and Harry and I coming up, both fired, when down it came to the ground, and was dead before my uncle reached it.

"A good day's sport, my lads," he exclaimed in high glee. "We shall soon have the waggons loaded if we go on in this way. Fred, you go to the camp to bring up the oxen to load with the tusks and meat, while Harry and I will look after the other elephants and the lion."

I had taken a good survey of the country, so that I believed I could find my way, and without hesitation set off. I had gone but a short distance when a troop of giraffes hove in sight, and beautiful objects they were, with their heads elevated on their long necks. Influenced by the propensity of a hunter I dashed forward in pursuit. Suddenly, my horse swerved on one side, and I saw that he had narrowly escaped a pitfall. Almost directly afterwards, two of the giraffes sank into other pits, and on turning round I saw that the animals were pursued by a party of natives, who had them thus completely in their power.

On examining the pit into which I had so nearly tumbled, I perceived that it was about twelve feet in depth, with a bank of earth about seven feet high left in the centre, broad at the bottom, and narrowing towards the top. The fore-legs of the giraffe had sunk into one side of the hole, the hinder legs into another, the body resting on the narrow bank, so that the creature in spite of all its struggles could not possibly extricate itself.

I left the natives to take possession, and rode on endeavouring to avoid the pit-falls, of which I had little doubt there were many on my way. I had, of course, to go much slower than I should otherwise have done. Though two or three times I nearly got caught, I safely reached the camp. Stopping merely to take some refreshment, I again set off with the oxen, to bring in the produce of our chase. We found that it was necessary to be quick about it, lest the natives should find that we had killed the elephants and appropriate the tusks. They, however, had hitherto been so busily employed in chasing the giraffes that they had not discovered the elephants. We took possession of the tusks, and as much of the meat as our party could consume.

Mr Welbourn had been almost as successful, having killed two fine elephants and a couple of deer. Next day we continued our journey northward. In passing over the plain, while Harry and I were riding on ahead, we caught sight of an animal occasionally rising out of the ground and then disappearing.

"That must be a beast caught in a trap or pit-full," said Harry; "let's go and see what it is."

"ALMOST DIRECTLY AFTERWARDS, TWO OF THE GIRAFFES SANK INTO OTHER PITS." [A. 169.

On reaching the spot we found that he was right in his conjectures. He told me that the animal was a quagga, which somewhat resembles a well-shaped ass. In vain the quagga tried to get out by the most desperate efforts. Sometimes its fore feet almost touched the top of the bank, but again and again it fell back.

"I should like to take possession of the animal," said Harry, "it doesn't appear to be at all injured, and if we could manage to break it in, it would make a capital riding horse. If you'll watch the pit, I'll go and get some of the men to come with ropes."

To this I agreed, and he soon returned with Toko and two other men, bringing not only ropes, but a large sack and a saddle.

"What are you going to do with those things?" I asked.

90

"You shall see," he replied. "It was Toko's idea."

The quagga looked very much astonished at seeing itself surrounded by human beings, and as before, it endeavoured to escape from the pit.

As it did so, Toko, who had fastened the sack to a loop at the end of a long stick, drew it over the quagga's head, so as to prevent its biting, which it would have done had it been able to see.

A halter was fixed round its mouth, and ropes were passed under its body, by which it was drawn out. As soon as it found itself on firm ground, it began to throw its legs out in all directions, but Toko held it fast by the halter. At last, wearied by its exertions, it stood perfectly still. The moment it did so, Toko made a sign to his followers, who clapped a saddle on its back, and drew tight the girths.

"Capital!" cried Harry. "I have got a first-rate steed at small cost, and I'll soon show you what it can do."

Before I could dissuade him from making the attempt, he, with his usual impetuosity, leapt on the quagga's back, and, seizing the bridle, told Toko to let go.

What Harry might have expected occurred. Off started the quagga, full gallop, towards the herd from which it had been separated by falling into the pit. I feared from the vicious nature of the animals, that, seeing some strange being on the back of their companion, they would kick it and its rider to death. In vain I shouted to Harry to stop his steed and come back: that was more than he could do. So telling Toko to mount his horse, I set off in pursuit.

The moment the herd of quaggas saw us coming, away they galloped at a furious rate. There were not many streams, but over the rocky beds of watercourses, through dense thickets, up hills, down valleys, on they went.

Our horses began to show signs of fatigue, and I was afraid Harry would be carried away into the wilderness. To attempt to throw himself off would have been madness, and yet while the quaggas were running, there was little chance that their companion would stop.

We had ridden so far that I knew our friends would be anxious about us, for they had not seen us disappear, and no one in the camp would know what had become of us.

To abandon Harry was not to be thought of, and we therefore pushed forward in the hopes of at length coming up with him and stopping his wild steed. The difficulty was solved in an unexpected way. Suddenly in front of the herd of quaggas appeared a large party of people armed with spears and darts. Uttering loud shouts, the blacks began to send their missiles among the herd. The quaggas were thrown into the greatest confusion, some going on one side, some on the other, others turning in the direction from which we had come. At length the shouts and cries around it brought Harry's quagga to a standstill, and enabled us to get alongside. I advised him to dismount.

"No, no!" he answered. "I have got my steed and intend to him, and if you ride near he'll go well enough."

Harry was right. The brute, pretty well tired out, went with perfect quietness, and submitted to be tethered with a strong rope and hobbles round its legs, so that there was no chance of its breaking away.

"I'll tame him!" cried Harry. "Tell them, Toko, no one must on any account bring him food—I alone will give it him."

By this time the natives, who had killed half-a-dozen quaggas, had come close to us. We considered that it would be prudent, if not an act of politeness, to thank them for stopping the quagga; and Toko, who was our spokesman, so explained matters, that

"OFF STARTED THE QUAGGA, FULL GALLOP." [p. 173.

the hunters expressed their happiness in seeing us, and invited us to their village.

We should have excused ourselves, on the plea of having at once to return to camp; but, as the day was already drawing to a close, and even Toko declared that during the darkness he should be unable to find his way back, we accepted the invitation, and set off with our new friends, who were in high spirits at the thoughts of the quagga flesh they were about to enjoy.

Their huts were larger and cleaner than any we had yet seen; and we found that, although the people were hunters, they were also agriculturists, and possessed pretty extensive plantations at the back of the village.

The women were immediately set to work to prepare the feast; and in a short time the whole population was banqueting. We, of course, soon knocked off, and begged permission to rest in one of the huts. We had scarcely however gone to sleep, than we were aroused by a tremendous hubbub; and, rushing out, we found all the women on foot, engaged in seizing their children, whom they had hauled out of their beds, or rather up from the mats on which they lay, and were belabouring them unmercifully with rods. On enquiring the cause from Toko, he told us that news had been brought that an immense herd of elephants was approaching the plantations. The object of beating the children was to frighten away the animals. This was, for one cause, good news for us, as we hoped to obtain full cargoes for our waggons. We at once offered to go out and shoot the elephants, if the natives would guide us to the trees in which we could take up our posts for the purpose.

We soon found plenty of volunteers, and, guided by them, we each reached a tree in the neighbourhood of the plantations, near which they assured us the elephants were sure to pass. We gladdened their hearts by telling them that they should have the meat, provided we retained the tusks for our share. The noise, however, continued; the women shrieking, and flourishing their rods, the children howling, dogs barking, and the men shouting at the tops of their voices and waving fire-brands. Our fear was that the elephants would be frightened, and turn back; but scarcely had we climbed up the trees, each of us accompanied by several natives, than we caught sight, through the gloom, of the dusky forms of an immense herd of elephants emerging from the thicker part of the forest. We at once, taking aim at the leaders, fired, hoping to kill some and turn back the rest. Two fell, and the herd halted, apparently too much astonished to tell what had happened.

This gave us time to reload, when again the animals came on, passing by the fallen bodies of their companions. Taking steady aim we again all fired; and, beyond our most sanguine expectations, three more elephants sank to the ground, each shot through the head. Whether or not the shrieks in front distracted their attention and made them regardless of the sound of our shots, I cannot say; but the animals scarcely stopped for a moment, though some of them trumpeted notes of alarm, and advanced with

"THE WOMEN SHRIEKING, THE CHILDREN HOWLING, AND THE MEN WAVING FIREBRANDS."
[p. 178.

apparent caution. The rest stopped lazily, waving about their huge trunks.

I was very thankful that we were high enough up the trees to be out of their reach. Though several passed, us before we had reloaded, others followed, and three more bit the dust. Neither did this stop the onward course of the elephants; for, breaking down the fences which enclosed the plantations, they swept across, seizing the fruit with their trunks, and transferring it to their mouths.

Again and again we fired together. The cries of the inhabitants did not stop their advance, though it tended to turn them on one side, where, meeting with several huts, they trampled them down as if they had been built of cards. Had it not been for the exertions of the people, the whole village would have been destroyed; which Toko assured us, had frequently in other instances been the case.

As soon as the elephants had passed, we descended, and as they showed no inclination to turn back, we pursued them, firing as we could make certain shots, thus killing I am afraid to say how many more, lest my account might not be credited.

The remainder of the herd then swept on, though we would not give up the chase until we had expended nearly all the ammunition we had with us. At length we returned to the village, where we found the people taking the loss of their crops very philosophically, as they considered that the abundance of elephant meat would make them ample amends.

"I hope the poor people will not get a surfeit," remarked Harry. "I suspect in a few days they'll wish the carcases at Jericho, or at all events, at a distance from their village. Our horses and the quagga would have fared ill, had the elephants come across them."

After a few hours' rest, we bade our friends goodbye, and mounted our steeds, promising to return for the tusks, which we reminded them were ours.

Harry wisely kept a sack over his animal's neck, and Toko and I rode on either side to guide it. The creature went wonderfully well, and sooner than we had expected we came upon the waggons. The news we brought was highly satisfactory, and without a moment's delay the oxens' heads were turned in the direction of the village.

The people received us as old friends, and to encourage them to help us we promised them a reward for each of the tusks they brought in. They had already begun to butcher the elephants which had fallen in their plantations, and in every direction round the huts strips of flesh were hung up to dry, creating an odour far from pleasant. They lost no time in bringing in the tusks. Harry and I were highly complimented on our performance. The tusks being cleaned and stowed away, our waggons were nearly full: another day's successful hunting would enable us to turn our faces westward. We accordingly promised to reward our hosts if they would bring us information as to the direction the herd had taken. Harry and I had been congratulating ourselves on the prospect of a quiet night's rest in our tent between the waggons; but we had not been long asleep when we were aroused by a tremendous clap of thunder which seemed to break directly over our heads, while almost immediately afterwards, there came a most fearful shrieking and shouting from the village close to which we were encamped. Slipping on our coats, we hurried out. As we did so a curious sight met our gaze. The whole of the male population were on foot, armed with bows, and arrows; and as the lightning darted from the black clouds we saw them shooting away at them as fast as they could place their arrows to the string.

As may be supposed, we kept carefully behind the savages lest we might be struck by the arrows, which we had heard were poisoned. The thunder rattled and roared, the lightning flashed, and the men shrieked and howled. I asked Toko what it all meant.

"They're shooting at the storm-clouds to drive them away," he answered.

"Do you think it will produce that effect?" I asked.

"Who knows?" he replied. "They fancy so, and are therefore right to try and get rid of the storm, and drive away what they believe would do them harm."

I told Toko that the powerful Being who rules the heavens would not be influenced by such folly, though he would be ready to hear the prayers of the smallest child. He seemed to take the matter far more lightly than I should have expected.

"They are poor ignorant savages," he remarked, "who have not the advantage of living with white men."

"SHOOTING AT THE STORM-CLOUDS TO DRIVE THEM AWAY." [p 182.

The storm swept by, and the poor people were satisfied that their shooting had driven it away.

Next morning, inspanning at an early hour, we proceeded in the direction we concluded the elephants had taken.

While camping at noon, some of the natives who had gone on ahead as scouts, brought us the satisfactory intelligence that the herd were feeding in a wood about eight miles off; and that as a stream ran by, they were certain to go down to drink in the evening; when, if we took proper measures, we should be able to kill as many more as we wanted. We lost no time, therefore, in proceeding onward, and as the ground was pretty level we made good progress.

We camped at a part of the stream where we could draw water; and where, from the rocky character of the bank, the elephants were not likely to come down and drink. On one side it was a swamp, between which and our camp we could leave our horses at liberty to feed, one or two men only being required to watch them. As soon as these arrangements were made, we set off to search for the spoor of the elephants, so that we might place ourselves in ambush on one side, as we had before done, to shoot them as they approached or returned from the water.

As we made our onward way, we caught sight of numerous elephants feeding at their ease in various directions. If they were part of the herd which we had lately attacked, they had soon recovered from their alarm. We took up our posts in satisfactory positions, hoping that,

"A COUPLE OF HUGE RHINOCEROSES."   [p. 187.

before the night was over, we should have bagged the full complement of tusks we required.

I do not suppose the detailed account of our various proceedings would prove interesting. Suffice it to say, we were not disappointed. Harry, I, and Toko shot one elephant apiece, and my uncle and Mr Welbourn each shot three, they using explosive bullets, which never fail to kill the animals they wound.

At length, frightened by the destruction of their companions, the remainder of the herd retreated, and we, leaving the bodies until next morning, returned to our tent.

As Harry and I were pretty well knocked up with our exertions of the previous day, we remained encamped while natives were employed in bringing in the tusks.

After breakfast we strolled out with our guns, hoping to get some wild fowl in the marsh, for we were somewhat tired of feeding on elephant's flesh.

We had killed several birds, and on our way back we stopped to look at the horses and quagga, which were feeding in perfect harmony. The latter having a bandage round its eyes, and it being hobbled, Harry went up to it, and spoke gently in its ear.

"Take care!" I exclaimed, "he'll give you an ugly bite."

As I spoke the quagga turned his head and very nearly caught him by the arm.

It was a lesson to Harry not to pet his favourite in future, and I advised that he should muzzle it until its temper should become softened.

We were standing talking, when suddenly the horses began to prance and kick up their heels.

"Hallo! what are those?" exclaimed Harry, turning round.

We then saw, emerging from the marsh, where they had been wallowing, a couple of huge rhinoceroses, who seemed to look upon the horses and us as intruders they had a right to drive off their domains.

It was not without some difficulty that we got out of their way. Clumsy as the animal looks, and short as are its legs, it can move with wonderful rapidity over the hard ground.

As our guns were only loaded with small shot, it would have been useless to fire at them. The horses could take pretty good care of themselves, though they exhibited their fear of the savage-looking creatures by scampering off in all directions.

Meantime, having withdrawn our small shot, we were ramming down bullets as fast as we could. Although the horses could escape, the poor quagga, with its legs hobbled and its eyes covered, had but a poor chance. The leading rhinoceros had singled it out as the object of attack; and, before Harry and I could fire, rushing furiously forward, it pierced the poor animal through with its formidable horns, pinning it to the earth. When too late to save the quagga, we both pulled our triggers, when the animal, still dragging the body of its victim on, rushed forward several paces before it dropped.

We, of course, reloaded, but before we could fire, the other rhinoceros might be in the midst of the camp and commit all sorts of damage. Fortunately, at that moment, Toko, who had just arrived with a party of men carrying the tusks, his rifle being loaded with ball, with a well-directed shot prevented the catastrophe we feared by killing the rhinoceros just before it reached the waggons.

We had an evening of rejoicing, for by the addition of our rhinoceros horns, our waggons were piled up to the very top; and my uncle expressed some apprehension that the axles might break down with the weight of the unusual load before we arrived at the coast.

We lost not a day in proceeding thither. On reaching Walfish Bay, we safely embarked the valuable produce we had collected.

So ended the first series of my adventures in Africa. I have, however, since made several other expeditions to various parts of that hitherto little-known continent, of which I may some day give an account to the world.

The End.